THE BLACK ROCK MURDER

WATERFELL TWEED COZY MYSTERY SERIES:
BOOK SIX

MONA MARPLE

For Lisa
Thank you for seeing the worst of me
And loving me anyway

1

———

"Go on, tell her." Cass repeated.

Sandy gazed between her best friend's eager face to Olivia's own coy smile. The three of them had been sat in The Tweed nursing hot chocolates for the last hour while an awful storm raged outside. Olivia had been a bundle of nervous energy, and had already spilled one mug of hot chocolate all over the weathered table when a crack of thunder raged outside.

Cass had pushed her to share her announcement, and she seemed uncomfortable.

"She doesn't have to if she's not ready." Sandy said, not wanting to see the girl embarrassed. "It's fine Olivia, tell me when you're... when the time's right."

Olivia looked at her, all doe-eyes, with relief.

"Oh, don't be silly." Cass said. "Shall I tell her for you?"

Olivia gave a snort of dismissive laughter and took a gulp of hot chocolate, for courage perhaps. The drink left a faint chocolate moustache above her upper lip. Sandy caught Cass' eye but they managed to conceal their amusement.

"Right, okay... it's not really big news..." Olivia began, but her attention was lost when the door to the public house opened. Her boyfriend, Derrick, launched himself at their table, and Sandy realised why she had been reluctant to share the news. It hadn't been nerves, but the fact that for Olivia, the most important person hadn't yet arrived.

"Evening ladies." Derrick said. He flashed a smile at them both, then planted a kiss on Olivia's forehead and took a seat. "Anyone need a drink?"

"Oh for goodness sake, we've been waiting for this moment all night! Don't distract her now." Cass said. Sandy noticed that some of her eyebrows weren't actually hair and hoped her friend wouldn't try to convince her to try out the microblading. "Come on, Livvy, it's a school night after all."

Olivia's cheeks flushed and she narrowed her eyes towards her big sister.

"Well, it's nothing that exciting really, I didn't even want to do an announcement like this. I've got a job, that's all."

"A job?" Sandy repeated. "That's great! Well done, Olivia! What is it? Where?"

"Well done Livvy, I'm proud of ya." Derrick said. His whole face was taken over with a smile, transforming him into a caricature of teeth and pride.

"It's in the church, helping the vicar." Olivia said, her voice quiet, posture rigid.

"That's wonderful." Sandy said. Rob Fields was a calm, kind man.

"The church?" Derrick asked.

Olivia nodded and crossed her slender arms over her chest.

"I didn't know you were religious."

She shrugged, in that sullen way teenagers had of

suggesting that nothing much holds any importance to them.

"Olivia..." Cass began.

"It's just a job." Olivia said. "Probably just filing papers and stuff, but I want to earn my own money. I don't want to cost you money, Cass."

"Enough, don't talk like that. We're family. And anyway, I look after you now, you return the favour when I'm old."

Olivia pulled a face. "I'm not making any promises!"

"I can't believe you're working in a church." Derrick muttered. Sandy glanced at him, saw the confusion on his face.

"Why?" She asked.

He shrugged his shoulders then in an action that mirrored Olivia's own. Was the shrug the international language of the teenager, Sandy wondered. "Just surprised." He said.

"Well, I pop in there sometimes on the way home from school..." Olivia admitted.

Cass raised her eyebrows, the hairs and the non-hairs.

"It's dead peaceful in there. Rob chats to me a bit sometimes, other times he just leaves me be." Olivia said. She grew self-conscious as she spoke and looked around at her audience. "I guess I just like it."

"Listen." Cass said. "There's nothing to be embarrassed about. You can go to church, you can believe in God or not believe in God... but if you're going to be a Christian, be a loud and proud Christian. In fact, here's a life lesson for you. Whatever you're going to be, be loud and proud about it. Life's too short to worry about whether everyone else agrees or likes the same things."

"I'm a Christian." Derrick admitted. He flashed a smile

at Olivia. "That's why I was surprised, cos not many people my age seem to believe..."

"And I'm not a Christian." Cass said, the bluntness of her words surprising Sandy. "But I'll always support you finding your own way and your own beliefs, sis."

"What about you, auntie Sandy?" Olivia asked.

Sandy considered the question. Like many of the villagers, she attended the church regularly for funerals and events, but she wasn't a devout attendee. "You know, I don't really know what I believe, to be honest."

"And that's ok too." Cass said. "Now, why don't the two of you walk home? I need to speak to Sandy but I won't be much longer."

Derrick nodded and stood up. Olivia did the same and planted kisses on Cass and Sandy's cheeks, then the two of them walked out of the pub hand in hand.

"Are you okay for money?" Sandy blurted when they were alone.

"Erm..."

"With Olivia saying she wanted to earn her own money, I just wondered if things were okay. Is business doing alright?"

"The salon's fine." Cass said dismissively. "We've had a few arguments about pocket money, but nothing major. She wants to buy some really bloomin' expensive make-up, it's gorgeous, but I don't have eyeshadows as expensive as the ones she likes and I work full-time! I said she could do some hours in the salon, but next thing I know she's been asked to help Rob Fields."

"Well he's a great person for her to spend time with." Sandy said.

"Yeah... I don't really know him."

"Me either, actually." Sandy said. "He comes in the shop for watercolour painting books. I like him."

"You like everyone." Cass said with an eye roll. It was true that Sandy got on with most people she came across.

"So, what did you need to speak to me about?"

"Oh, Sand, you won't believe it." Cass said. She buried her head in her hands dramatically.

"How's my favourite lady?" Tom Nelson called as he appeared at their table. Sandy shot him a look that she hoped told him it wasn't a good time. Her best friend had already had her moments of appearing unsettled by Sandy's blossoming romance with Tom. He was a catch, with his tall good looks, but he appeared unable to recognise subtle cues, and leaned in to kiss Sandy, who avoided his mouth and instead whispered *not now* in his ear. He pulled away, puppy-dog sadness on his beautiful face, and Sandy's heart ached as she felt the opposing pulls on her from him and Cass.

"We're just in the middle of something." Cass said, her voice laced with a false friendliness.

"Ah, girl talk." Tom said. "Say no more."

Sandy watched him skulk away to behind the bar, where a queue had formed during his absence. She let out a sigh. "You really could be nicer to Tom, you know."

Cass blinked at her, heavy spider lashes suggesting she was more surprised by the comment than it warranted. "I just miss you, Sand. But you're right, I'm sorry. Anyway... can I talk to you now?"

"Of course you can." Sandy said. "What's going on?"

"It's Tommy Fisher."

Sandy let out a laugh, then saw the serious expression on Cass' face. "Bomber? That's a blast from the past... what about him?"

"He's been messaging me."

"How?"

"Facebook." Cass admitted with a frown. "It's my fault really, I was on there one night and I thought I'd look some people up, you know how you do... I looked up loads of people, not just him. He's not changed, you know. Well, he has obviously, but if you could guess how you'd expect him to look..."

"I'd expect him to be Mr Flash." Sandy muttered. "Toned, tanned and... I can't think of another T. Covered in designer clothes, probably."

"Have you looked him up too?" Cass asked, face solemn.

"No, I have not!" Sandy said, appalled. "Why would I want to look up the guy who broke my best friend's heart?"

Cass nodded. "Well he does look just how you said."

"On her sixteenth birthday."

"I know..."

"But?"

"But what?" Cass asked.

"But he's been messaging you, and you've been replying, haven't you?"

Cass blushed. "I might have sent the first message."

Sandy groaned.

"What?! Hear me out... he was my first love, Sand. I was just curious. Thought I'd see what he's been up to."

"And what has he been up to?"

"He says he's never stopped loving me, Sand." Cass said.

"Of course he does." Sandy said. She rolled her eyes.

"I know, I know. Look, if I was you, I'd be saying all this too. I've been so nervous about telling you."

"Just don't do anything stupid." Sandy warned. "You've always fallen in love too fast. Don't let him fool you into...

into... don't let him break your heart again. Where is he anyway? What's he doing with his life?"

"He's an entrepreneur." Cass gushed.

Sandy groaned.

"He's successful, Sand. You should see the photos. Ooh, let me see if I can..." Cass pulled her mobile phone from her handbag and tapped away at the screen, then held it up for Sandy to see. She gazed at the face of Bomber, looking slightly older but unmistakably him. Could a man who had barely changed on the outside have changed on the inside?

"He looks just as I'd expect." Sandy said, noting the deep tone of his skin and the designer logo on the polo shirt he wore.

Cass flicked to another image. Bomber in front of a red sports car that cost more than Sandy's cottage.

"I've seen enough." She said, and Cass returned the phone to her handbag. "So, you're messaging each other. What's the point of it?"

Cass gave a sad smile and shook her head. "There isn't a point, is there? I'm just reminiscing, I guess, thinking what could have been."

"What could have been if he hadn't been a complete moron to you, don't forget that bit." Sandy said.

"We were kids!"

"He broke your heart." Sandy said, her voice stern. "I was there, remember. I was there trying to put it back together for you. Watching you waste your tears over that waste of space. Argh! I can't believe you're having anything to do with him."

Cass nodded and wiped a tear from her cheek. "I'm sorry, I shouldn't have..."

"You shouldn't have dug it up." Sandy said. "Sometimes

you have to leave rubbish where it belongs. And Bomber was nothing but rubbish."

"He was rubbish that I loved." Cass admitted, and Sandy realised that her friend needed support, not scolding. She reached across the table and gripped Cass' hands in hers.

"I know." She murmured. "I know. Just leave him alone, yeah?"

Cass forced a smile and nodded.

2

*T*he floor was soaked.

Every time a customer walked in, the wind forced a splatter of rain and mud in with them and the people already gathered in the cafe's warmth drew their cardigans tighter around their bodies and shivered.

"This is madness." Bernice muttered as she returned to the kitchen with the mop under her arm. "I can't keep up with it. Someone's going to fall their length out there if we're not careful."

"It's going to have to stop soon, isn't it?" Sandy asked, gazing through the kitchen towards the front door, where she could glimpse the dark skies and hear the roar of heavy rain on the pavement outside. The storm had begun early the evening before, just as Sandy was about to head out to The Tweed to meet Cass and Olivia, and the village had been barraged with an onslaught of rain, fierce winds and thunder and lightning since.

"The news says it'll be like this all day." Bernice said as she washed her hands. The kitchen was radiant with the smell of honey and lavender, a new recipe that Sandy couldn't wait to try. As if reading her mind, Bernice opened the oven door and pulled a tray of two circular cake tins out. The top of the sponges were slightly dark, just how Sandy liked it, and Bernice had already prepared a buttercream frosting to go between the two layers.

"That smells so good." Sandy said.

"Hmm." Bernice grunted. "Two minutes too much oven."

Sandy smiled. Bernice was never happy with her own creations in her strive for perfection. Luckily, the customers all seemed to realise how talented she was and how delicious her cakes were.

"I'll take this out." Sandy said, picking up the bacon sandwich she'd just prepared. She'd popped down to help with the serving because of a sudden influx of customers; a great problem to have. It seemed that all of the villagers had come out despite the awful weather, a phenomenon that was common in Sandy's experience. People tended to notice the bad weather and fight against the feeling of needing to hide out in their own home, so braved the weather and hid out in Books and Bakes instead. The awful, wet days could be some of the busiest for the cafe, and Sandy expected she would be needed for most of the day downstairs in the cafe, leaving her beloved books upstairs unsupervised. It wasn't an ideal situation, but she was a valuable extra pair of hands to make sure customers didn't wait too long for their orders.

She carried the bacon sandwich out to the cafe and smiled at how busy it was. There was a spark of energy amongst the customers as they all shouted across from table to table, competing to see who was the most wet and who had the least sleep the night before thanks to the storm.

All of the lights were on and they flickered with each bolt of lightning, causing the customers to gasp and watch the bulbs. One woman tugged on the sleeve of her coffee date every time it happened, and the man jerked her off of him so he could continue eating his full English.

"Here you go." Sandy said, placing the food in front of Dorie Slaughter, who sat with her son Jim. He was already in his police uniform, the wet shirt stuck to his bulging stomach. "No food for you, Jim?"

"Not today." He said, seemingly oblivious to the fact that he looked as if he was competing in a wet t-shirt competition. "I've got to head to the station in a minute."

"We're talking about Elaine." Dorie shared between chews of her breakfast. "Her birthday's coming up soon, you know, and you know what my Jim's like. He goes over the top. I'm telling him nothing too special for her."

Sandy let out a small laugh. Dorie had a love/hate relationship with her son's partner, at times appearing to have welcomed her into the family, at other times fiercely jealous of Elaine's place in her son's affections.

"Don't laugh, Sandy, this is very serious. My Jim has spoilt women all his life and look where it's got him. They stay for the good times and then, poof, take advantage and abandon him." Dorie continued.

Jim shifted in his seat uncomfortably.

"What did you want to get her, Jim?"

He let out a deep sigh. "I was thinking we could have a weekend away, go across to the seaside for a night maybe."

"With your shifts!" Dorie exclaimed. "No time to sit and eat breakfast with your mother but you can find time for a weekend away. Nonsense."

"You're probably right." Jim agreed. He was a peace-keeper, a timid man who hated confrontation. "Your idea was better anyway, mum."

"Of course it was." Dorie said. "I know women."

"Dare I ask?" Sandy said.

"I'm getting her a steam iron." Jim said.

"A steam iron?" Sandy repeated. "Has she asked for one?"

Dorie let out a small, mean laugh. "She buys clothes that are meant to be crinkled, that one. But that's no good for my Jim's shirts. She's dating a respectable man now, there are certain standards she needs to keep."

Sandy tried to hide the smirk from her face. Elaine Peters had remained single since her husband had died years ago, and yet Dorie talked about her as if she was a harlot who cavorted with all types of questionable men.

"So, a steam iron so she can iron your shirts." Sandy said. "She's a lucky lady."

With that, she walked away before Dorie realised she was being sarcastic.

Her sister, Coral, was in the middle of taking an order from an elderly woman, so when the doorbell rang out to signal another customer, Sandy instinctively looked up with a smile to welcome them.

Her smiled dropped when she saw who had entered.

Even without having seen the pictures the night before, she would have recognised him instantly.

"Well, I'll be damned! You workin' here, Sandy?" Bomber called out, his voice as brash and irritating as it had always been. Sandy cringed. There had been a time, many years before, when she had managed to tolerate him. But that had changed when he broke her best friend's heart. Now, even the sight of him, the mere ring of his voice, made her furious.

"Coral, I'll leave you to serve." Sandy said with a hiss. Her sister looked up at the harshness of her words but nodded her agreement as Sandy stomped out of the serving hatch and through the cafe, then up the stairs.

The quiet of the books was a welcome relief to her. She padded through the shelves, looking at the books, rearranging some that had been misplaced by the day's browsers, until her breathing returned to normal.

Her reaction to seeing Bomber was extreme, she knew. But Cass' devastation years earlier had been extreme too, and Sandy had been there for every part of it. Cass' parents hadn't seemed interested at the time, distracted by a furious silence that had filled their house at that time. Of course, Sandy realised, calculating the years in her head, it was around that time that Cass' father had been having the affair that produced Olivia. At the time, Sandy had only known that Cass was heartbroken and had nobody else in the world to turn to.

"Oh, hello, Rob." Sandy said as she glanced down one aisle of books to see the vicar flicking through a huge art book.

"Sandy!" Rob said. He gave her an easy smile and she wished for a moment that she was as comfortable in her skin as the vicar appeared to be in his. "How are you?"

"I'm fine." She lied. "I hear you've offered Olivia some work."

He closed the book so his full attention was on her. "Yes... I need some help. I haven't been blessed with organisational skills, I'm afraid."

Sandy smiled to herself, remembering the state of his house on the occasions she had visited. "She's a good kid, I'm sure she'll do well for you."

"Everyone needs a second chance, after all." Rob said.

His words, and the direct implication of them towards Sandy's reaction upon seeing Bomber, made her jump. "What?"

"Everyone needs a chance." Rob repeated. "Are you okay? You look like you've seen a ghost."

"No, no, I'm fine." Sandy assured him. "I'll leave you to it."

She walked away and took a seat behind the till, where she loaded up the computer and checked the reports from the previous day's sales. To her constant amazement and delight, the bookshop sales continued to increase week by week. Her large space allowed her to stock a wide range of specialist titles, and word of mouth was attracting dedicated readers from far and wide.

"Sandy." A voice came, distracting her from her work. She glanced up, not needing to, to see that Bomber had followed her upstairs.

"What?" She asked, making no attempt to hide her dislike for him. Tanned, toned and not to be trusted, that was all she needed to know about Bomber.

"Wow, it's good to see you too!" He said. Sandy noted the gold rings on his fingers and the heavy Rolex draped on his wrist.

"I've got nothing to say to you, Bomber." She said. "If you have to come in here, someone else can serve you."

"Look, I know I did wrong, will you just hear me out?"

"No." Sandy said. It struck her that if Bomber had broken her own heart she probably wouldn't still be as angry with him as she was for the hurt he had caused Cass. "Just get out, please. And don't look for Cass. She's better off without you."

"You make her decisions now, do you?" He asked, a sneer across his face.

"When she's not thinking straight, I help her remember certain things. And I know for sure she's better off with you in the past where you belong." Sandy said.

Heat took over her face as she became more and more angry.

Rob Fields appeared from the aisle he had been perusing and looked over in her direction, his face etched with surprise and concern. "Everything ok?"

"Yes." Sandy said as she crossed her arms. "This gentleman is just leaving."

"Sandy..." Bomber pleaded, his tone still light with the arrogance of a man used to getting his own way.

Sandy was distracted by the sound of footsteps stomping up the staircase. Coral appeared at the top of the stairs, her face white.

"Sandy, it's happened again." She called, then turned and ran back downstairs.

"Excuse me." Sandy said, following her sister. Her heart sank as she wondered what might have happened. Some of the kitchen equipment had been temperamental. She should have replaced things before now. It was nicer looking at the plump balance of her business bank account than paying money out for equipment that could possibly last another month, though.

The cafe was a congregation of silence with Dorie Slaughter leading the flock. She glanced across at Sandy and cleared her throat as a boom of thunder roared across the sky.

"Don't be alarmed, ladies and gentlemen." Dorie called, then trotted across the cafe to Sandy's side.

"What's going on?" Sandy asked.

"Gurdip."

"The shepherd?"

Dorie nodded, then proceeded to fold her arms across her chest so each hand was resting on the opposite shoulder. As if she were dead.

"Dorie!" Sandy exclaimed, horrified.

"It's a dangerous job." Dorie said with a shrug. "I thought I should tell people so they take care on their ways home."

"I don't understand..." Sandy said.

Dorie rolled her eyes and repeated the dead person act. "Died in the storm. Fell off Black Rock, last night my Jim says. We all need to be careful. Nobody knows the lay of the land better than a shepherd."

"He's dead?" Sandy asked. She didn't know Gurdip at all, other than by sight. She'd spot him standing atop a hillside with his flock of sheep occasionally, but he had never been in the cafe.

"Awful business." Dorie said, removing her arms from her chest to Sandy's relief. "But, you work with nature, and nature will remind you it's stronger than you."

"I can't believe it." Sandy said. Black Rock was a high ledge looking out across the beautiful Peak District valley on the edge of the village. By daylight, it was a popular place with couples, a romantic viewing platform, a place remote enough to offer privacy despite its popularity. In the dark, it was a terrifying, uneven base, with an invisible drop that promised certain death. Sandy shuddered at the thought of tumbling from the ledge, realising the fate that lay ahead, and being powerless to stop it.

"Careless, these young ones." Dorie said. She shook her head. "He shouldn't have been there."

Sandy nodded her rare agreement with Dorie. Surely it was common sense that Black Rock would have been the worst place to go near during such an awful storm.

The customers had begun to return to their conversations. Coral watched her closely, awaiting orders.

"I'm going to stay upstairs." Sandy said. "Just try and

stop Dorie treating this place as her own personal platform to announce things, please."

"Yes, boss." Coral said, with a resignation that suggested she knew she was no force at all against Dorie.

Sandy sighed and returned upstairs.

She sat at the till, continued reading the sales reports, and only realised some time later that Bomber had disappeared.

3

———

*D*orie remained in the cafe after closing, while Sandy wiped the tables down and Coral did the takings. She watched the women work as Bernice and Derrick cleaned the kitchen. As Coral put her coat on and prepared to leave, Dorie made no attempt to move.

"Are you staying for the night?" Sandy teased.

Dorie shook her head. "My Jim's coming to get me."

"Oh." Sandy said. "Do you know what time?"

"Nobody's got the commitment these days, everyone shuts at 5 exactly and forgets all about work. It wasn't like that when I was working. You stayed as long as it took."

Sandy rolled her eyes towards Coral. "It's ten past six, Dorie. And I'm not kicking you out, but I do have evening plans..."

"Off with your fancy man?" Dorie asked.

Sandy felt her cheeks flush. "No, actually."

"Hmm. I know when I'm not wanted." Dorie said. She stood and pulled on her leopard print coat and a bright pink wool hat. The door burst open before she could pull on her gloves. "Ah, here he is now. My Jim has a job that needs him until late, you wouldn't understand."

Sandy followed her gaze. Jim looked exhausted.

"Goodness, Jim, are you okay? Shall I get you a drink?"

The police officer shook his head and collapsed into a chair across from Dorie.

"Woman hater, that's what you must be." Dorie muttered under her breath. "It was all 'come on, off with you' for me, but my Jim walks in and suddenly drinks are on offer."

"Jim?" Sandy asked. He looked entirely spaced out.

"It's been a long day." He admitted. Sandy had always imagined his career to be a strange choice for such a nervous man, making every day a leap outside of his natural comfort zone, but it seemed as though he had found a role that allowed him to do little actual policing work. He spent much of his time on the front desk rather than out dealing with crime.

"Are city back?" She asked. The city police had been sent across several times recently to investigate the spate of unconnected murders that had plagued the usually peaceful village. Their presence was unwelcome, and their determination to keep Jim out of the investigations had frustrated him.

"City?" Jim asked.

"I heard about Gurdip." Sandy explained, then gave a look towards Dorie. "Your mum shared the news."

"That's what I've been doing all day." Jim said. "Let's just say you don't want to fall off Black Rock. What a mess."

Sandy felt her stomach churn.

"Why would city be back, though?" Jim asked.

"Oh, I don't know, they seem to like it here!" Sandy attempted a joke.

"It's not a murder." Jim said. "You know that?"

"Well, my source wasn't exactly official..."

"I'm as official as you can be next to the police themselves." Dorie exclaimed. "My Jim gives me good information."

"I didn't tell you about Gurdip." Jim protested, palms open.

"It's ok, son, Sandy understands."

"Is it just an awful accident, then?" Sandy asked.

Jim nodded. "There was no visibility last night, with the rain and the wind. Tragic really."

"And you've been dealing with it?" Sandy asked, hoping the surprise she felt wasn't audible in her words. If the police department had trusted Jim Slaughter to deal with it, they must be giving the death very little attention.

Jim nodded. "A dog walker rang it in and there was nobody else free so I went across to have a look. I thought it'd be flytipping or something. I'll be happy to get back to neighbour complaints and paperwork, trust me."

"Oh, now, you do important work. Don't talk like that." Dorie said. She rubbed her son's arm.

"Come on, we should get going. Elaine's going to have a pie ready for us all." Jim said as he checked his watch.

"I hope she's followed my pastry recipe this time." Dorie said, then looked at Sandy and lowered her voice conspirationally. "Shop bought!"

"It sounds like you've earned that dinner." Sandy said, ignoring Dorie.

Jim pushed his chair back and rose to his feet, his stomach knocking into the table as he stood. He let out the groan of a man approaching middle-age and Sandy pretended not to have heard.

"I'm too old for this." Jim said, with a sad shake of his head.

Sandy noticed that Coral was still hanging around by the front door in her coat, and exchanged a worried glance with her as Jim and Dorie walked out of the cafe. Coral locked the door after them, then scratched her head.

"I've never seen Jim so down." She admitted.

"Me either." Sandy said. "It must have really shook him up today."

"Maybe he should rethink his career." Coral said, with a shrug. "The occasional dead body is a hazard of the job surely, as a cop."

"I don't know." Sandy said. "I think he's so used to city stomping in and taking over the serious cases. Whatever it is, he probably just needs some time to process it. Poor Gurdip."

"Did you know him?"

Sandy shook her head.

"He was nice." Derrick said, emerging from the kitchen with Bernice.

"Were you two hiding out until Dorie left?" Sandy asked.

"We couldn't possibly say." Bernice said, casting a wink in Derrick's direction.

"How did you know him?" Coral asked.

"He caught me sleeping in a barn a while back, when I'd just left home. He pretended he'd not noticed me. Next night, I thought I'd try my luck again, and he came out with some food for me. Sat and had a chat with me for a bit."

"Oh, that's nice."

"Yeah. Nicer than the other guy, that's for sure."

"What other guy?"

"The farmer whose barn it was. He found me that

second night after Gurdip had gone. Kicked me out, literally. I had the bruises for weeks."

"That's awful." Sandy said. "Who would do that?"

Derrick shrugged and walked across to the front door. "I'm gonna get going, see you all tomorrow."

"I'm coming too." Bernice said, and waved bye as she walked out of the cafe with Derrick.

Sandy looked at Coral, who had been ready to leave for some time but still stood in front of her. "What's up?"

"Your plans tonight." Coral said, a grin spreading across her devious face. "What are they?"

"Oh, for goodness sake, Coral, can't I have any secrets?" Sandy asked with a laugh. "I'm going to a yoga class."

Coral burst into a fit of laughter and Sandy shook her head and pulled on her own coat. "Thanks for your support."

"Yoga? I'm sorry, but why?"

"There's a leaflet on the noticeboard, I just thought why not. You could come?"

"Nah, you're alright." Coral said. "I'm going to have fish and chips and watch junk TV all night."

"Hmm." Sandy said as they turned off the lights and walked out into the storm. "That sounds a much more appealing idea, actually."

"It's always the way. These things sound like a good idea when you book them, but after a long day at work, all you want to do at our age is go home and relax."

"At our age?" Sandy exclaimed.

"Mm-hmm."

"Coral, we're in our 30s!"

"Exactly, things aren't the same as they used to be. Anyway, enjoy yoga... if you actually go." Coral said. She set off towards the fish and chip shop, leaving a damp Sandy on

the pavement outside the shop. Any possibility of her skip-
ping the yoga class had disappeared. She would prove Coral
wrong.

She pulled the hood of her yellow mac over her head
and began the walk to her car, keeping her head down to
stop the rain attacking her bare face.

"Where's your boat then?" A voice called.

"Ha bloody ha." Sandy called into the storm. Several
people made fisherman jokes about her yellow mac, and
they were starting to wear a bit thin. She didn't have the
patience for them in this weather.

"Ah, she does still have a sense of humour then." The
voice came again, closer to her, and recognisable. Sandy
glared at the man who had fallen in step beside her.

"I've already told you, just leave me alone." She said as
she reached The Tweed. Her car was parked on the road
outside.

"Just give me ten minutes?" Bomber pleaded. Sandy
sighed. She had a choice of speaking to the man who would
not apparently leave her alone until she did, or going to the
yoga class she didn't want to attend.

"Fine." She agreed, and stormed into the pub. Tom
Nelson smiled when he saw her, then watched in confusion
as she took a seat and Bomber sat across from her. "Go on,
what's so important."

"Well..." Bomber began. He fiddled with one of the
thick, gold bands on his fingers. "I don't know where to start.
How have you been? You're working in a bookshop, eh,
that's nice."

"I own the bookshop." Sandy said, immediately hating
herself for boasting. She had nothing to prove to anyone
and especially not someone like Bomber.

He let out a low whistle, pretending to be impressed.

She wanted to punch him. "I'm an entrepreneur too. They say the first million's the hardest but it's the most satisfying too, yeah?"

Sandy glared at him.

"Right, well, I only arrived last night... place hasn't changed at all, has it? Been away years and then it seems like you've never left."

"What are you doing here?"

He grinned, revealing unnaturally white teeth. "I think you know that."

"Cass." Sandy said.

Bomber nodded. "She's bloody gorgeous, isn't she?"

"You haven't grown up at all, have you?"

"Ah come on, I'm being nice. I mean, she was always a looker, even under all that make-up, but she's something else now."

"You had your chance."

"I was a kid." Bomber said with a shrug. "I made a mistake, I know that. But then she reached out to me and I was blown away, I mean I never thought she'd forgive me."

"She shouldn't."

"She has, though." Bomber said.

"She's told you that?" Sandy asked.

Bomber flashed a wicked grin. "Let's just say the messages we've shared, they're... well, there's no animosity now."

"You're disgusting." Sandy said. "Have you even apologised to her?"

"I've begged for her forgiveness, and she's given it. I don't have to be here sitting with you, ya know. I'm here because you matter to Cass."

"Well, I'm not asking you to be here so don't expect a thank you."

Bomber sighed. "You're like a little Rottweiler or something."

"I care about my friend, and I know you're bad news."

"Well, let's see what she says."

Tom appeared by her side and she was glad to see him, grateful for his strength near her. "Are you okay, darling?"

She nodded as he planted a kiss on her forehead.

He held out a hand to Bomber. "I don't think we've met?"

Bomber eyed Tom and shook his hand. "I'm an old friend of Sandy's."

"You're no friend of mine." Sandy said. She was so furious her body was shaking. "And you've had your ten minutes."

"Oh Sandy, don't be like that." Bomber said. "I'm going to see Cass now, and I'd like to be able to tell her me and you have sorted our differences out."

"You'll never be able to tell her that." Sandy said. She glared at him. "We're done."

Bomber shook his head and stood up, then stormed out of the pub.

"Wow... remind me to never get on your bad side." Tom said. He took Bomber's seat and reached across the table to hold her hands. "Who is he?"

"The man who broke Cass' heart."

"I didn't know she was dating." Tom said.

"Not now, when we were younger. He was her first love."

"And you're still holding that against him?" Tom asked. His earnest expression made her lose her breath. The suggestion that her anger towards Bomber was irrational took her by complete surprise.

"Well, yes. I'll never forgive him." Sandy admitted.

"Hmm." Tom said.

"What?"

"I don't know the story, Sand, so I don't really want to get involved... it's not my place to have an opinion. But, from the outside, it kind of sounds like it's not your forgiveness to give."

---

4

*T*he day dragged.

Sandy snapped at Derrick for taking a little over an hour for his lunch break, then remembered he'd had a medical appointment and apologised profusely.

"I've survived worse." He said with an easy grin. "Is everything okay?"

Sandy had nodded, told him that she had slept badly and felt as grouchy as a bear without honey. It wasn't a lie exactly. She had slept badly, and she did feel grouchy. But it wasn't the whole story.

She was still furious with Bomber for returning to the village, annoyed with Cass for contacting him in the first place, and troubled by Tom's refusal to see her side. Was she really overreacting? It wasn't her heart that had been broken, after all. But surely, that's what friends were for? To say when something was a bad idea. To warn you away from repeating the same mistake.

As if she didn't have enough on her mind, she'd arrived at work that day to a request for a home visit to discuss a catering job.

"Oh, no." She'd said after Bernice had finished relaying the voicemail message.

"I know, pet, it won't be easy." Bernice said as she tucked a strand of auburn hair behind her ear. "Want me to come with you?"

It was a generous offer. Bernice much preferred being behind the scenes than dealing with customers. Sandy would have liked her support at the appointment but didn't want to ask that much of her. "Thank you, but no, I'll go on my own. These appointments are always hard."

Her stomach churned at the thought, but she couldn't say no. There were no other catering businesses in the village, and she wouldn't see a Waterfell Tweed resident forced to contact an out-of-town company for something so personal.

No, she would have to go.

She tried to put the appointment to the back of her mind while she served the steady stream of customers in the bookshop.

Rob Fields returned and bought the art book he perused the day before and, to Sandy's relief, didn't mention her altercation with Bomber. A chapter of the U3A arrived at lunch time and their group of sprightly pensioners explored the aisles with wild glee, every single person buying at least two books before heading downstairs for coffee and cake.

As they made their way downstairs, Felix Bartholomew, also in his autumn years, appeared from one of the aisles at the back of the store with a mischievous twinkle in his eyes.

"I had to hide out in case they thought I was one of them and forced me onto their coach!" He exclaimed, casting furtive glances around the bookshop to check that the coast was clear.

Sandy laughed. The older man, with his extravagant moustache and fabulous collection of bow ties, was revealing himself to be quite a character. "You're safe now, Felix."

"If you see Dorie, make sure she knows I wasn't speaking to any women up here. I think she's the jealous sort."

"Really?" Sandy asked with a smile. Dorie had been laughing off Felix's marriage proposals for weeks, ever since he began renting her cottage.

"She's playing hard to get but she likes that I've only got eyes for her." Felix said, and Sandy realised that in his younger years he must have been an attractive man. There was a charming sparkle in his eyes, and his face still had a marvellous bone structure.

The conversation raised her spirits, but when she was locking up the cafe and should have been able to look forward to burying her nose in her latest mystery novel while enjoying a hot bubble bath that The Cat would no doubt perch on the edge of, she instead had to walk across the village square for a meeting with a widow.

Anastasia was an unknown to Sandy. A woman who had followed her husband across the country, from Leicester to Waterfell Tweed, to allow him to follow his dreams of becoming a shepherd. She was plainer than her name suggested, as if all of the creativity and flair had been used up in naming her and left none over for her personality or appearance. Her hair was grey with hints at the caramel colour it had previously been, and her house was as ill-maintained as her.

She opened the door to Sandy only after seven knocks of increasing volume, as if she hadn't requested the appointment and specified the time. Her eyes were hollow shells, ghosts walked in her pupils and she shielded her face from the day light.

"Come in." She said in a gravel voice as she allowed Sandy to enter the smoke-filled home.

Sandy let out a cough, the stale cigarette fumes catching in the back of her throat. She allowed herself to be led down the old-fashioned corridor, all floral wallpaper and a radiator sporting bright blue, chipped, paint.

"This is the best room." Anastasia croaked, and Sandy looked around and nodded her approval. An old TV stood in the corner of the room, it's depth twice the size of it's screen. A dining table sat against the window, covered in a yellowed lace tablecloth. An open fire was unlit, the mantelpiece around it heavy, solid wood. Above was the centrepiece of the room, an enormous photo of Anastasia and Gurdip on their wedding day. Anastasia grinned into the camera, her hair very much caramel, while Gurdip gazed at his bride in adoration.

"That's a beautiful photo." Sandy said.

It was the wrong thing to say. Anastasia began to weep immediately, reaching down the bosom of her top, past the delicate gold cross hanging from a necklace, to retrieve a wad of tissue paper that she pressed against her eyes to physically prevent the tears from escaping.

Sandy said nothing. There was nothing she could say.

Anastasia looked as confused by life as she should. She had supported her husband, agreed to begin a new life, and that new life had ended cruelly. Gurdip stolen by the very land he had devoted himself to.

"Sit." Anastasia commanded, and Sandy took a seat at the dining table. Her attention was caught by the garden beyond the window. A lush green lawn was bordered by a well-ordered and intricate array of flowers, plants and shrubs. An apple tree stood in the centre of the lawn, and a shabby chic bench sat beneath the tree. The contrast between the house and the garden made Sandy smile. Anastasia and Gurdip were clearly both more comfortable outdoors.

"So, I, erm, thank you for considering me for the wake." Sandy said, the words clumsy on her tongue.

Anastasia shrugged. "There isn't anyone else, is there."

"Erm, well, no... right, ok. What we normally do is..." Sandy began. She opened the brochure that she had brought out with her, and laid it flat on the dining table. She had ordered the brochure be printed a few weeks earlier, so that her catering prices were written in black and white. It was easier for her to show someone a price than tell them it. She hated the feeling of bargaining with someone and asking for money from them. Especially when she was profiting from someone's death.

"I don't want what you normally do." Anastasia said. She too was captivated by the garden, and stared out at the lawn with an expression Sandy couldn't read. "I want something for him, something that will make people think of my husband. Not just another buffet."

Sandy bristled at the words, then reminded herself that she was with a grieving widow. She pulled out a notebook and pen from her handbag and turned to a blank page. "Okay, what are you thinking?"

"You tell me." Anastasia said. "I'm not much of a domestic goddess. I don't know what flavours go together, or anything."

"Well, I have to admit I didn't really know Gurdip very well."

"Nobody did." Anastasia spat, then recovered and smiled at Sandy. "I'm scared that nobody will go to the funeral."

"Oh, you don't need to worry about that." Sandy reassured her. The villagers of Waterfell Tweed never missed a funeral. She was confident that most of the locals would be in attendance, dragging their black outfits from their wardrobes and adopting their morose expressions. A good funeral could be the highlight of the village week.

"The wake needs to be right for him." Anastasia insisted. "I have to do this last thing for him."

"Okay." Sandy said. "Okay. Well, what were his favourite foods?"

"Lamb." Anastasia said, a small, dry laugh erupting from her. "Before he was a shepherd, of course. He couldn't eat it any more when he got to know the flock."

"Can I ask, what made him want to be a shepherd?"

"Oh..." Anastasia said, and her eyes lit up for the first time. "A boyhood dream. He couldn't even tell me why, just that as long as he could remember, it was what he wanted. Of course, his family, they made all of the children go into medicine."

"He was a doctor?" Sandy asked.

Anastasia nodded. "An excellent one. He was so calm and reassuring. He was the same with the flock. We managed to put some money away, both of us climbed the corporate ladder for years and we lived a pretty meagre life. We were just happy together. Tending our garden, growing our own food, going to church. There's only so much you can spend in a garden centre, the rest we saved."

"You didn't have children?" Sandy asked.

Anastasia's face clouded over. "No... we... I couldn't."

"I'm sorry, that was a tactless question." Sandy said. She felt her cheeks flush.

Anastasia said nothing, lost in her thoughts as she looked out on her garden.

"You grew your own food? Maybe I could incorporate that into the food I make." Sandy said.

"Maybe." Anastasia rasped.

"What did you grow?"

"Strawberries, they were his favourite. Do you, do you want a tour?"

Sandy nodded, unsure whether the tour would be of the house or the garden. To her relief, Anastasia led her to the back door, and out into the fresh air. The kitchen garden wasn't visible from the best room, Sandy realised, as Anastasia led her down the lawn and then out towards the right hand side, where a small potting shed stood. Behind the shed, row upon row of plants were revealed, each row neatly labelled.

"This is amazing." Sandy said. She had never seen anything like it.

"These are the potatoes. Buggers, they are." Anastasia said. She was transformed out of the house; her posture tall and proud, her eyes bright. "I call them the needy children... they take up so much time, and space. But there's nothing like a potato salad with my potatoes in it."

Sandy looked at her quizzically.

"Gurdip did the cooking." Anastasia explained with a coy smile.

"Maybe I could make some of his recipes? The potato salad?"

Anastasia nodded but her expression was vacant. "I can't believe he's gone."

Sandy reached out and placed a hand on the woman's shoulder as she descended into tears.

"It was an awful, awful accident." Sandy soothed.

"No!" Anastasia exclaimed, recoiling from Sandy's touch

as if it had burnt her. She turned to Sandy, fury on her face. "Don't you ever say that. It was no accident."

"He fell, didn't he?"

"He knew the land like the back of his hand. He wouldn't have fallen. He wouldn't be so careless. It wasn't an accident." Anastasia insisted. She was almost hyperventilating, her breath coming in ragged, short bursts. "Don't let anyone say that."

"Okay." Sandy said. "Okay. It's just what I heard. I'm sorry, I really didn't mean to upset you."

"People need to know the truth." Anastasia whispered.

"Look, I've got enough ideas to start working on. I can really use this vegetable garden as the inspiration and make a really nice, fresh selection of food. Would that be ok?"

"Of course." Anastasia said. "That's all I want."

"I'll see myself out." Sandy said. She left Anastasia in the garden, looking out over her beloved kitchen garden, and made her way back through the smoky house. It was a relief to return to the fresh air and finally be able to make her way home. Even more than earlier, she was desperate for that hot bath, although she knew she wouldn't forget the widow's grief easily.

Gurdip fell, Sandy thought as she crossed the village square and tried to ignore the hard feeling in her stomach.

5

*D*espite the call of the hot soak, Sandy was sufficiently unsettled by her visit to Anastasia that she headed left instead of right, barging into The Tweed where she hoped Tom would be able to speak to her. Gus Sanders almost fell out of the door as she pulled it open, his eyes glassy, cheeks ruddy.

"Evening!" He called, for he was a pleasant drunk.

"Good evening, Gus. Heading home?"

"See if dinner's in the dog." He joked, giving a mock salute as he stumbled past her and turned towards the cottage he shared with his wife Poppy, Tom's sister.

The commotion attracted Tom's attention, and from behind the bar he met Sandy's gaze. He was in the process of pulling a pint and she caught his uncensored joy at seeing her walk in. Her stomach flipped and she wondered if her own face revealed how fond she was of him as she trudged across the pub towards him.

She took a bar stool and allowed him to finish serving his customer, and then a second customer who had waited patiently for their turn. He made pouring a pint seem like an art form. The way he applied just the right pressure to ensure that the golden liquid was dispensed evenly, leaving a small head at the top of the glass, sitting atop a pint of opaque amber.

"Mocha?" He offered, turning his attention to her finally. She rarely drank, preferring the creamy warmth of a mocha instead, and was constantly touched that Tom had began to stock the sachet drinks behind the bar when he realised that.

"Yeah, go on then." She accepted. "I was heading home to see The Cat but I wanted to see you."

Tom cocked his head to one side. "Sounds ominous."

"I was just missing you." Sandy said, which wasn't entirely true. She was perfectly happy at the thought of a night in on her own until Anastasia had unsettled her. "And I wanted to talk to you... if you have a few minutes?"

Tom surveyed the pub, checking every cosy nook with his eyes as he vigorously stirred her hot drink. There was an art form to perfecting her drink of choice too; lots of stirring to ensure the powder mixed properly, and then a top up of hot water as the initial water always sank after stirring. "I'm on my own so I can't leave the bar, but you can prop it up and keep me company. I've had much worse bar flies."

Sandy laughed. The idea of her propping up a bar was out of character. "Sure, I'll stick around for a while. Have you had a good day?"

Tom nodded in between drying glasses. Sandy felt uncomfortable sitting relaxing while he worked.

"Can I help with that?" She asked.

"Nah, don't be silly. There's not many left. Tell me about your day. What's on your mind?"

Sandy took a deep breath. "I've just been to see Gurdip's widow."

Tom stopped and gazed at her then, his full attention on her in his usual, intense way. "How is she?"

Sandy shrugged. "I want to say not coping, but she must still be in shock. We're catering the wake. Those meetings are never easy, but..."

"You're worried about her?"

Sandy nodded. "She said some things that I found concerning."

"Like what?"

"She's adamant he didn't fall."

"What?" Tom asked, his brow furrowed. "I didn't think there was any question about that."

"Neither did I." Sandy admitted. "There's no investigation, it's just been ruled as a natural cause of death. That's what I've heard, anyway."

"Hmm." Tom murmured. "I guess it's natural to look for answers."

"I think in her mind he's this superman figure who couldn't have been hurt by the land. She won't believe that he could have fallen, even in the storm. Not on the land he knew so well."

"Well..." Tom began.

"What?"

"It wasn't land he knew so well."

"What do you mean?" Sandy asked. Sure, he was a first generation shepherd, but he wasn't a newcomer. He'd had plenty of time to grow accustomed to the rolls and contours of the Waterfell Tweed countryside.

"Black Rock wasn't his patch." Tom explained.

"I don't..." Sandy stuttered, realising how little she knew about the work Gurdip did.

"Shepherds have to stay on their patch." Tom said.

"Black Rock wasn't his. I thought it was odd as soon as it was announced, that that's where he was found."

"Could he have got lost in the storm?"

"I guess so." Tom said. "It's just odd, because he had the shelters on his own patch. It would have been quicker for him to head for one of those than end up at Black Rock."

"Well, like I say, if he lost vision, he could have been entirely lost."

"Must have been, I guess." Tom said with a shrug. He wouldn't argue the point.

"I might go out there." Sandy said. She took a sip of her mocha and felt the satisfaction of the velvet smooth texture. "Fancy joining me?"

"Sure." Tom said, too quick, too easy. He flashed her a boyish grin. "I've been waiting for you to suggest it."

"You haven't?" She exclaimed with a laugh. "How did you know I would?"

"Like I say, something just doesn't sit right with me. I'll pick you up at 10am?"

"Tomorrow?" She asked, unused to this version of Tom who was headstrong with her. She quite liked it.

"No point waiting." He said, and then leant across the the bar and planted a kiss on the tip of her nose.

"I love you, Tom Nelson." She said, with a smile.

"I love you." He said, holding her gaze for a moment too long, until a customer stood further down the bar coughed their impatience. "Oops, back to work."

"I'll leave you to it, The Cat will be furious with me." Sandy said, climbing off the bar stool and turning to leave.

As she walked towards the door, she could see inside one of the cosy booth seats, hidden from view on the walk towards the bar. To her horror, Cass sat in there, uncomfortably close to Bomber, who appeared to be talking at a million miles per hour. Cass, doe-eyes, spider lashes, listened intently to him until, sensing someone nearby, turned her head and spotted Sandy.

"Oh, hey Sand." Cass said, uncomfortable. "Erm, want to join us?"

"Yes, I think I might." Sandy said. She sat opposite the two of them and watched the smile drain from Bomber's face.

"Is that the time?" He asked, with a glance at his watch.

"Don't leave on my account." Sandy said, her voice a sheet of ice, imploring him to do the opposite.

"I'll have a few more minutes." Bomber agreed.

"We've just been catching up." Cass explained. "Bomber's done ever so well for himself, you know. Got a whole team of people working for him."

"Is that right?" Sandy asked. Bomber smiled at Cass but said nothing. "What do you do, exactly?"

"Jack of all trades, I reckon." He said. "I follow the money."

"Hmm." Sandy said, concerned by his vague answer.

"Sandy, we're just catching up, stop the interrogation." Cass said with a laugh, attempting to change the mood.

"Cass was telling me about her salon. I always knew she'd go far."

Cass beamed at his flattery. Sandy tried not to roll her eyes.

"And you." Bomber said. "The bookshop and stuff. I mean, you girls are really doing well."

"Yes, we are." Cass said, and raised her wine glass for a toast nobody else took part in. Bomber's pint glass was empty and Sandy had left her half-finished mocha on the bar. "Here's to the three of us, business owners! Who'd have thought it."

Sandy gave a half-smile.

"Right, I'm going to go." Bomber said. "Leave you ladies to it."

"Aww." Cass grumbled. "We were having fun."

"We can carry this on another time." Bomber said to her with a wink, and her cheeks flushed red. He stood, gave a half-wave to them both, and left.

"Geeze, he makes me cringe. Please tell me you're not being sucked in by all of that." Sandy said.

"Sandy." Cass said, a warning in her voice. "You have to back off and let me make my own decisions."

"Back off?" Sandy challenged.

"Sorry... that came out harsher than I meant." Cass admitted. "But you do need to let me make my own decisions."

"Mistakes."

"Maybe. But it's my mistake to make."

"You know he arrived back in town on the day Gurdip died?"

"He didn't actually, it was the day after, and what has that got to do with anything, anyway?"

Sandy swallowed. "He told you it was the day after?"

"Erm." Cass began. "I saw him the day after and he said he'd just arrived."

"It was the day Gurdip died, trust me."

"And?"

"And there's suggestion - this is just between me and you - that it might not have been an accident."

Cass's eyes widened. "Another murder?"

"I don't know. I'm going to look into it."

"Hold on." Cass said, her eyes narrowed. "Are you suggesting Bomber had something to do with it? Because it's a big jump from someone who was a bit of a rogue as a teenager, to being a murderer."

"I know." Sandy admitted. She wasn't ready to level the accusation at Bomber... yet. "But he's hiding something."

"Like what?"

"I don't know. But I'm going to look into that too, Cass. I need to protect you."

"I'm an adult, Sand." Cass said, but her voice faltered.

"What did he tell you tonight? He was clearly boasting, but did he give you any specifics?"

Cass looked to the side, replaying the conversation. A smile crossed her lips. "He wanted to talk about me mainly. I had to force the information from him about himself... oh, not like that, he's just shy. Modest."

"Or sketchy."

"Look, we're not going to agree on this. He isn't hiding anything. He's just found me after years, and he wanted to get to know me again, not talk about himself. Isn't that sweet?"

"Possibly." Sandy said. She glanced at her own watch. She needed to go home. "Just be careful."

"Yes, mum." Cass teased. Sandy rolled her eyes.

"You know I'm just worried about you, Cass, don't you?"

Cass looked up at her and Sandy realised how much effort she had made for this meeting with Bomber. Her foundation was thicker than normal, her face contoured to within an inch of it's life, creating hollow cheeks and sculpted cheekbones. Cass was a wizard with a make-up set. Her eyelashes, always heavy with black mascara, seemed gravity-defying.

"I don't want to be on my own." Cass admitted. "I'm ready to settle down, not play games. So, trust me, if Bomber has any tricks up his sleeve, I've got no time for them. I just... I never really got over him. He was my first love and, gosh, I saw him tonight and my stomach flipped. He's not your type, I know that, he's too loud and flash, but under all of that, he always had a good heart."

"If that's true, why did he..."

"Because he was a kid!" Cass exclaimed. "I'm deciding whether I can forgive him. And that's my decision to make, Sandy, not yours."

The ghost of Tom's own warning rang out from Cass, and Sandy nodded her understanding.

"You're right. I'm sorry if I've been too overbearing." She said. "I only ever want to look after you."

"Oh, I know that." Cass said, a smile returning to her lips. "You're my best friend, it's your job to warn me about stupid mistakes. But, sadly, it's also your job to watch me run full speed ahead towards the mistakes, and then dry my tears when I've had my heart broken."

"I hope I don't need to dry your tears this time." Sandy said, as she reached across the table and squeezed her best friend's hand. "But I will if you need me to."

6

*I*t was a glorious sunny day, the visors in the car pulled down to protect their eyes from the intense beam. They drove through the outer streets of Waterfell Tweed, rows of neat cottages transforming to occasional farmhouses, a shabby B&B, and then the pavement itself disappeared and the land opened up to fields on each side.

Sheep grazed behind dry stone walls, their coats thick, spray painted to suggest an elaborate code by which the farmer could tell which ram had impregnated which ewe. Occasionally, they looked up at the noise of the car passing, but mostly they continued their feast, unperturbed.

"Nearly there." Tom said.

Sandy nodded, lost in her thoughts. They continued driving in silence until Tom indicated and pulled in close to Black Rock.

"I'd forgot how close it was to the road." Sandy said, as she unclipped her seat belt.

"It needs to be handy for the teenage couples to get to." Tom said with a grin. It was a famous kissing spot locally, although Sandy only knew that through the grapevine. No boys had invited her to Black Rock as a teenager, when she'd been awfully uncomfortable in her skin and had spent her evenings in her bedroom reading novels.

They climbed out of the car and walked across the grass towards the ledge. There was no police tape, no restriction on people coming and going from the area. Sandy stood as close to the edge of the ledge as she dared, forcing herself to look down at the drop.

"What a horrid way to die." Sandy said, the jagged bits of stone dotted around the drop making her wince. Poor Gurdip.

"It's hard to imagine the storm being so bad that he wouldn't make it to the road." Tom said, surveying the scene. The road led to a small, unofficial parking area, where people could either follow the public footpath across the fields, or admire Black Rock.

"It's not enough to turn this into a murder investigation, though." Sandy said. "Could it be suicide?"

Tom shrivelled his nose up.

"No, I don't think so either." Sandy admitted.

Tom stood next to her and took her hand in his. "I'd hate to lose you, you know."

She gave an awkward laugh. "I wasn't going to jump."

"Ha, ha. It just makes you think, standing here. I'm glad I found you, Sand."

"I'm glad too." Sandy said, and allowed Tom to kiss her.

"Get away!" An incensed voice called, and Sandy jerked away from Tom, worried that perhaps the scene was a police restricted area after all and she had failed to see the signs. An older man, in a flat cap and with a border collie trotting faithfully by his side, stormed towards them. "I said get away!"

"We're okay." Tom called, cheeks flustered pink. He moved away from Sandy and towards the man, palms outstretched, conciliatory. "We're being careful up here."

"Careful?" The man barked, his walking stick swinging by his side as he darted expertly across the land towards them. His scraggled beard glistened with sweat, or spit; it was impossible to tell which. "I don't give a rat's uncle whether you're careful. This is my land!"

"This is public land." Sandy countered, although her certainty came only from the fact that it was treated as if it were public land.

"Is that what they're telling people?!" The man exclaimed. He was just a few feet away from them now and Sandy saw that he had a whistle on a chain around his neck. His jumper had moth-eaten holes in, but she caught a glimpse of a shirt and tie underneath it. "This is my land. You're trespassing and I'm done with it. It's getting ridiculous. Go on, get away."

"I'm sorry." Sandy said. "Who are you?"

"I'm Victor Dent, and this here's my land." He said, gesturing across the car park (which was more a worn down strip of grass) and towards Black Rock. It was difficult to say how old the man was, with so much of his face hidden behind facial hair, but his eyes were a piercing blue, as if while the rest of him had aged his eyes had remained bright and youthful.

"Mr Dent?" Tom said. "There's a car park here, and a public footpath. We're entitled to be here."

The man groaned and fished around in his trouser pocket. Sandy glanced at Tom nervously. She wasn't sure she wanted to hang around and see what he pulled out. She'd heard her fair share of warning tales about incensed farmers shooting intruders. Shoot first, ask questions later seemed to be the motto for some of them. Tom, however, patiently watched the man dig through a collection of pockets without alarm, until Victor Dent found a large mobile phone. He swiped at the screen inexpertly and then held up a photograph of a map showing the boundaries of his farmland. "See? Now, get gone."

"I'm confused, Mr Dent. Why is there a footpath across your land, if you're saying it can't be used." Sandy asked, genuinely curious. She had directed many Ramblers and other holiday makers to the Black Rock trail for a day's walk, making her a definite contributing factor to the farmer's annoyance.

"Bloomin' council are useless. It's been going on too long, I won't stand for it any more. You are trespassers and trespassers get what they deserve. Understand?"

Sandy gulped and nodded, the words sending a chill down their spine, as Tom reached for her hand and led her away.

"We're sorry, we'll go." Tom said. They returned to the car and sped out of the car park as Victor Dent looked on menacingly.

**

They returned to Sandy's cottage, where The Cat looked at them with disgust for disturbing the peace before returning upstairs to Sandy's bed.

Sandy made her and Tom steaming mugs of tea to calm their nerves.

"We should call the police." Tom suggested.

"And say what? He's entitled to protect his land, surely." Sandy argued.

"How can Black Rock be his land, though? It's a public area."

"I might go to the library and check the records." Sandy said. She draped her legs up on the settee and let out a yawn.

"Tired?"

"I didn't sleep well." She admitted. "I don't know if I'm ready for another murder investigation."

"You think it's murder?"

"Like you say, it's odd that Gurdip was there in the first place. Maybe Victor Dent found him out there and lost his temper."

"I think crazy farmers come out with guns not photographs of their land map." Tom said.

"Yeah, that's a good point." Sandy said. "Although he wouldn't risk a second killing, surely. One man falling off Black Rock in the storm is a tragic accident, but if everyone who goes up there starts suffering the same fate, that's another story altogether."

"Maybe he thought Gurdip would act as a warning."

"It has done." Sandy explained. "I've heard plenty of people in the cafe say they'll be avoiding that area for their walks now."

"Why would he be so keen to keep people off his land?" Tom pondered aloud.

"Boundary disputes are brutal, Tom. Coral always told me they were the worst cases to report on when she was covering the courts for the newspaper." Sandy explained. Her sister had been a journalist before joining her to work at Books and Bakes. "Neighbours can get vicious with each other. I guess it's the same with farmers sometimes."

"I guess so." Tom said with a shrug. He glanced at his watch and jumped up from the chair, grabbing his coat as he did. "I've got to go, I didn't realise it was this time. Sorry, Sand!"

She let out a light laugh. "Fancy driving me in? I'll check on the cafe."

**

Books and Bakes was, of course, in no need of checking. Bernice ran a military operation always, just as her household had been ran as a child and how she had tackled the whole of life since. With expert planning, discipline, and a stiff upper lip.

The only sign of her busyness was the usual smear of flour that ended up highlighting her auburn hair.

"We won't even notice when you go grey." Sandy said as she joined her friend in the cafe kitchen. "We'll just assume it's the flour."

"When I go grey?" Bernice asked with a smile and a raised eyebrow. "You think this colour's real?"

Sandy gaped at her. She'd known Bernice as long as she could remember and she'd always been a beautiful redhead.

"Okay, close your mouth." Bernice laughed. "My hair really is this colour. But I might get a little help with the pesky white hairs..."

"I'm plucking mine out." Sandy confessed. The grey hairs were appearing quicker now, it seemed like every time she parted or brushed her hair, out sprung a long white tendril.

"Yeah, I did that at first too. Didn't want to face up to it.

Then I went to the hairdresser for a wash and cut, and she said to me, 'you've not got too many greys'! I was mortified. Then I figured if she knew about them she might as well hide them. Pulling them out isn't a long-term plan."

"True." Sandy agreed. When she pulled a grey out, she would have crazy visions of herself in six months' time, entirely bald.

"What do you want, anyway? I thought you were off all day." Bernice said, back to no-nonsense. She had a plan for the day and it didn't involve Sandy's presence.

"There was an interesting turn of events." Sandy said with a shrug. Bernice hardly reacted, she had no time for gossip or dramatics. "A farmer kicked us off his land, out at Black Rock."

"Victor Dent?" Bernice asked, without raising her head. She was scrubbing stubborn pieces of scone from a baking sheet.

"You know him?"

"You mean you don't?" Bernice asked. "Everyone's got a story about him, I thought."

"Well, I've got one now. What's yours?"

Bernice's cheeks flushed. "Oh, nothing really. I know the name, I could point him out for you, but he wouldn't know me."

"Hmm." Sandy murmured. "Did you think Black Rock was public land?"

Bernice stopped scrubbing for a second to consider the question. "I guess so. I've never really thought about it."

"I need to find out more about him." Sandy said.

"Why?"

"Gurdip was on his land when he died." Sandy explained.

"But it was a natural death."

Sandy shrugged. "His widow is adamant it wasn't an accident, and I've got this feeling. What she's saying makes sense. Black Rock is so close to the road. Would an experienced shepherd like Gurdip really get so lost in the storm that he'd fall from there?"

"It's definitely strange." Bernice agreed. "But people die in strange situations all the time. Did you see that someone set their head inside a microwave with concrete the other week? He didn't die somehow!"

Sandy did a double take at the change of subject. "Who would concrete their head in a microwave?"

"I think his name was Bill." Bernice said, her attention firmly focused on the washing up once more.

Sandy smiled to herself and left her friend to it.

She needed to discover more about Victor Dent, and she knew exactly where to turn.

7

*S*andy arrived at Books and Bakes early, her trusty notebook stashed away in her handbag ready to begin questioning people about Victor Dent. She had slept fitfully, her body refusing to warm up so she climbed out of bed twice in the night to add additional blankets. When she woke, foggy-headed, to her alarm at 6am, she saw there were no blankets at all on the bed. Her nighttime wanderings to the closet must have been dreams. Her duvet had been tossed to the floor and The Cat had padded such a cosy looking sleep chamber into it that she had left him, and the duvet, in that position when she left for work.

Arriving at the cafe, she flicked on the lights and turned the radio on a low volume to keep her company. Thoughts of Gurdip, his hard-working honesty, flicked at the edge of her mind but she pushed them away and gathered her ingredients.

She kneaded dough to prepare a shortcrust pastry, mixed the frozen fruits she had pulled from the freezer the day before, mixed up a cherry jam that smelt devine, and toasted flaked almonds before sprinkling them on the finished Cherry Bakewell. She slathered slices of bread with good-quality butter on both sides, arranged them in a heavy dish, sprinkled sultanas, a sugar mix, and then a mix of whisked eggs and milk, then added a dash of cinnamon before placing the bread and butter pudding in the oven and hungrily inhaling the scent.

Baking in the morning was a dangerous occupation. In the first two years of owning the cafe, Sandy's waistline had spread as much as word of mouth, until she managed to control which cakes she sampled, and how big the sampling pieces were.

Now, she focused on the other senses that baking required. There was nothing quite like the scent of bread and butter pudding, spicy and rich, or the tactile experience of kneading dough.

There were so many things that machines could do now. No need to mix your own dough, slice your own ingredients, or wash your own dishes. She'd happily never wash a dish again, but there was a magic involved in chopping, mixing and measuring. Experimenting, just a little. Adding a touch to the cake that told people, *this is my creation.*

The toasted flaked almonds, when all of the recipes called for simply flaked almonds, created another flavour sensation. A taste dimension that surprised and delighted the foodies. An unexpected piece of heaven, on a plate, in a little cafe in Waterfell Tweed.

Sandy took another deep inhale, as the door unlocked.

Bernice flashed her a grin. The only other person who truly understood the joy of arriving early and creating food for others to savour.

"Smells good." She complimented. "I do love your Bakewell."

Sandy smiled to herself, and despite her restless sleep

and the weight on her shoulders, she knew that Books and Bakes was still her sanctuary. Whether she was in the kitchen baking, or upstairs tending to her books, the place gave her calm. Centred her.

"Thanks, B." She said, and walked through to the cafe to add the Cherry Bakewell to the highest cake stand in the display case.

The bell rang out as she did, and in walked Dorie Slaughter, her hair such a pale lilac it was hard to tell whether the new shade was intentional or not. Her bottom half was fit ambitiously into a pair of lycra yoga pants, her top half swamped in a bright pink t-shirt that commanded "RELAX!".

"Good morning Dorie, look at you." Sandy said with a grin.

Dorie glanced down at herself, as if she had forgotten what she was wearing, which Sandy doubted was possible of that outfit. Dorie's tiny feet were adorned in trainers, and judging by the fact that she had been in the cafe for almost a whole minute and hadn't said a single word, she seemed to be out of breath.

Dorie took a seat at the table closest to the counter and picked up a menu, despite being a daily customer and probably knowing the offerings better than Sandy herself did.

"Shall I get a tea ready for you?" Sandy called across.

Dorie nodded, jowls of fat below her chin bobbing up and down.

Sandy poured a huge mug of tea and then, on the spur of the moment, poured a tall glass of cold water and delivered both to Dorie. Dorie took the water and glugged it all in one, letting out a grateful *ahh* afterward.

"What do you fancy?" Sandy asked, hovering at Dorie's

table with her order-taking notebook and pencil poised ready.

"What's... *healthy*?" Dorie barked, as if ejecting the word from her mouth as far as she could.

"Erm, well, I'm no expert..." Sandy admitted, aware of the small muffin top overhanging her own trousers. "But poached eggs are supposed to be, I think? Or scrambled eggs."

"Ugh." Dorie curled her nose up. "I'll have a full English."

"Okay." Sandy said, hiding her amusement. "Are you on a health kick?"

"Elaine's idea." Dorie said. "She reckons we all need to get a bit more exercise, watch what we eat. If you see her, tell her I had those poachers eggs."

Sandy giggled. "Your secret's safe with me. I'll call it data protection..."

"Very good. Well, go on, get cooking. I've walked all the way here and I'm famished."

Sandy retreated to the kitchen and placed the order with Bernice, then returned to Dorie's table with a second glass of water for her.

"So, what's kicked off this health regime with Elaine?"

Dorie rolled her eyes. "My Jim had a check up and the doctor said he needs to lose some weight. Stupidly, my Jim told Elaine, thinking she'd comfort him, like I would have, you know, offer to make him a nice dinner like a woman should. Oh no, not Elaine. Now the house is like a lettuce farm and she's on at us both. Hiding car keys so we have to walk!"

"Oh, wow. I guess if it's for your health, though, Dorie..."

"Health, puh. I've got some padding, but my husband didn't have any and look what happened to him."

"What happened to him?" Sandy asked, realising the point Dorie was trying to make only once the words were out of her mouth.

Dorie shot her a glare. "He died, Sandy."

"Oh, yes. Sorry." Sandy said.

"Gurdip was too thin too. Thin enough for the wind to blow him off Black Rock, anyway."

"I wanted to ask you about that." Sandy said.

Dorie's ears pricked up instantly at the hint of gossip. "Well, of course dear, I am a font of knowledge as you know."

"I wanted to know about Victor Dent."

"Ooh look, breakfast's here!" Dorie exclaimed. Bernice placed the heaped pile of food in front of her. "Sandy, let me eat in peace for once? People are always wanting my time."

"Oh, of course." Sandy said. "Another time."

"Hmm." Dorie murmured, attention firmly focused on checking that Bernice had made perfectly runny egg yolks.

**

Victor Dent's name came up on its own that morning in the cafe.

Sandy was helping Coral make a particularly difficult order - a cappuccino with an extra shot. The science behind the request appeared to have baffled Coral, leaving her unable to do more than stand by and watch as Sandy pressed the cunningly disguised 'extra shot' button on the machine.

"Victor Dent's out being a menace again." A man announced to the cafe. Sandy turned to see that the voice belonged to Gus Sanders, the butcher, who was sat with his wife Poppy. She placed a hand on his arm, attempting to make him be quiet. "He should be keeping a low profile."

"The man's always been a menace." A villager who Sandy didn't recognise called across to Gus.

"Gus, is Black Rock public land?" Sandy asked.

The butcher puffed up at her question being directed to him, his chest growing taller and inflated. "Well, of course it is. Car park up there, public footpath entrance, it's for the good of the whole village that is. A place of beauty. We had our first date up there, didn't we, Pop?"

"Oh Gus." Poppy said, embarrassed. "It was hardly a Black Rock date. We went for a walk."

"You're wrong." Dorie called, empty plate in front of her, second mug of tea cooling down nicely ready to drink. "The land belongs to Victor Dent."

"Nah, it can't."

"It does."

"It can't, Dorie, you're mistaken."

"I can assure you I'm not." Dorie said. "That piece of land has always been in the Dent family."

"Why's there a car park then, eh?" Gus asked, showing off now. Sneering.

"There isn't a car park." Dorie said with a shrug. "It's grass that's been parked on time and time again."

"Alright then, why doesn't the dry stone wall come up to the road? Why leave the space for a car park?"

Dorie sighed. "Because it's on a bend without a passing place. Victor was tired of cars hitting the wall - nobody got hurt there but he was out repairing that one piece of wall every week. So he decided to move it back a little."

"That makes perfect sense." Sandy admitted. The bend

was lethal, with no visibility. To imagine it without the space that Victor Dent had created made her wince.

"Of course it does, it's what happened. And then all and sundry saw it as an open invitation to use his land. He's got every right to be annoyed."

"There's a code and he broke it." Gus called.

"Oh, for goodness sake. What code would you know about? Victor Dent is a good man. I'm not going to sit and listen to this rubbish." Dorie exclaimed. She rose to her feet and stormed out of the cafe.

"Oh Gus." Poppy said. She tapped her husband's arm and watched out of the window as Dorie began the trek back towards her home.

"Looks like old Dorie's got her eye on a new man." The unknown villager called out with a grin. Sandy glared at him. Dorie had remained faithful to her late husband's memory throughout the decades since he passed. But she had been unusually defensive of Victor Dent, and Sandy couldn't help but wonder why.

"What's this code anyway, pal?" The man called across to Gus.

"When you work the land, there's a code. You never see another stuck."

"Like those truckers who drive across frozen lakes? Always have to come to the help of another driver if they see one stranded? Even if they hate his guts?" The man called.

Gus nodded vehemently. "Exactly like it."

"What's that got to do with anything? You are talking rubbish, Gus." Poppy said. Sandy could imagine her eye roll. Poppy, the primary school teacher, dealt with children all day and yet gave the impression there was no bigger kid than her husband.

Gus sighed, splaying his hands across the table. "He was horrid to Gurdip."

"When?" Sandy asked, interest sparked.

"The night before he died." Gus said. "Gurdip got lost out there and old Victor Dent found him. He was in a bad way, Gurdip was, but Dent didn't help. Screamed at him, he did. Practically man-handled him off the land. Tells him, if he ever goes back on his land, he'll kill him."

A shiver ran down Sandy's spine at the words. "Are you seriously suggesting Victor Dent threatened to kill Gurdip the night before he died? How do you know that?"

"Gurdip himself told me." Gus said. "He came in The Tweed. Needed a drink to calm his nerves before going home. He was pretty shook up. Even, well, nearly," he paused, uncomfortable with the words, as if betraying an embarrassing secret, "nearly cried at one point. He was scared."

Sandy allowed the words to sink in as the customers continued their conversation.

"Sis." She whispered to Coral, who had seen the best and worst of life working as a journalist. "Killers don't threaten to kill, do they? Don't they just get it done straightaway?"

"Oh no." Coral said, breezily. She hadn't been listening to the conversation. "Some people threaten it for years and then one day they snap. You should always take a threat like that seriously. Why, have you upset someone?"

"No." Sandy said, her heart heavy. "But I think I've just found another murder to investigate."

8

*S*andy didn't so much as walk down the street to The Tweed, but storm there. She knew she should give Tom a reason to explain why he hadn't mentioned Gurdip's emotional visit there the night before his death, but she was furious. Red-faced, shaking fists kind of fury.

She barged into the pub, quiet in the lull between lunch and the evening, and physically collided with a startled Bomber, who managed to hold out his arms to catch her.

"Thanks... sorry." Sandy managed, thinking she really needed to start entering the pub a little slower, before she realised who the man was. "Oh, it's you."

"Always a pleasure to see you too, Sand." Bomber said with a grin. Sandy could imagine the women he'd flashed that smile at over the years, women who she guessed would have been flattered by it until realising his true colours at some later date. The trouble with Bomber, his attention felt captivating. When he was interested in you, he wasn't just interested, he was obsessed, infatuated. A true Romeo, with his cheeky grin and his guitar-playing. It was no wonder

Cass was falling under his spell again. "In fact, can we have a chat?"

Bomber gestured to an empty booth table.

Sandy shook her head, but a glance at the bar showed Tanya alone, duster in hand, attempting to look busy. She let out a resigned sigh and followed Bomber to the seat, planting herself down on the plush, padded seating.

"What is it?" Sandy asked.

Bomber grinned and tilted his head to the side, like a curious dog. "Will you ever give me a second chance?"

The honesty of his question stunned Sandy for a moment, her mouth open like a goldfish before she composed herself. "What does it matter to you?"

"Haven't you ever made a mistake, Sand?" He asked, his tone low. He fiddled with his hand as he spoke, picking at the skin around his thumbnail. "I know I blew it big time and Cass didn't deserve it."

"I don't lie awake thinking about it, don't worry. It's not like it's controlled my life for all these years." Sandy said. "I just don't want her to get fooled by you again."

"I couldn't believe it when she popped up and messaged me." Bomber said.

"Something we agree on, finally." Sandy allowed.

Bomber glanced at her, earnest, hopeful, and Sandy was transported to their teenage years. She'd spent almost as much time with Bomber as she had Cass while they were dating, Cass having told him that the two of them came as a package deal. She smiled involuntarily at a memory of him buying them each a Valentine's Day present, a typically extravagant gesture - a dozen red roses for each of them. Cass had shrieked with delight while Sandy had accepted her bouquet with confusion, until Cass had explained that she had warned him not to dare buy something for just one of them.

"We had some good times too, eh?" Bomber said, as if reading her thoughts.

She nodded, unable to deny the memories. The lazy summer afternoons spent on the park, seeing who could swing highest. If she concentrated, she could remember the queasy feeling in her stomach as she swung higher and higher, the dread and excitement of wondering if the swing might do a full loop and wondering whether, if it did, she would be able to hold on. If her best friend back then had been Cass, and if Cass and Bomber came as a package deal just like she and Cass did, then surely Bomber had been her best friend too.

"Oh my." Sandy murmured, with a gasp. She had thought she was acting so decently, so selflessly, remaining angry on her friend's behalf. In actual fact, she was furious with Bomber because she had lost him too. He had betrayed Cass, and disappeared from both of their lives.

"Everything ok?" He asked, an eyebrow raised.

"I just remembered... we used to get on pretty well, didn't we?"

Bomber nodded slowly. "I missed you nearly as much as Cass. Don't tell her that."

Sandy scrunched up her nose. "I won't be keeping any secrets for you!"

"It was a joke."

"I know." Sandy said, running her fingers through her hair as a rowdy group of men in hi-vis jackets entered the pub. "I was so busy being angry at you I forgot how close we were."

"You guys were the best." Bomber admitted with a smile.

"I mean, you drove me crazy at times, both of you, but I don't think I've ever had better friends."

"Hmm." Sandy said, not ready to give up the hard anger in her chest. "And yet you still hurt us both."

Bomber pursed his lips and Sandy flinched, although she couldn't have said why. He had never been violent, never had a flash of temper, even as a teenage boy with a body full of raging hormones. "I did."

"I'm sure we're not here to go down memory lane, so what's up?"

"I just want to..."

"In fact, you've had control too much. Let me do the questions." Sandy said, pushing the memories from her mind. This was what he did. Mind games, smooth talking, a smile at the right moment. She refused to believe it. "Are you going to hurt Cass again?"

Bomber sighed, weary. "I hope not."

"You hope not?" Sandy asked, incredulous. "Are you serious?"

"I don't even know if she might give me a second chance, Sand. She cares way too much about what you think of it all. But if she did, I don't know, we're not teenagers any more."

"What does that mean?"

"It means back then we had these dreams about how life would be, and now we're paying bills and changing the bedsheets. I have no idea what this Cass wants from life, or if there's a way I could fit in to that."

"She wants the same things she ever did." Sandy said without a pause. She knew her friend's deepest hopes better than Cass herself probably did.

"She used to want me."

"She used to have you, and you had your chance. Don't

you dare start thinking you're the only one who can make her happy, settle down with her. She's an amazing woman."

"I know that better than anyone." Bomber said.

Tanya appeared at their table, her long dark hair hanging in a plait over one shoulder. "Are you guys needing drinks?"

"No." Sandy said.

"Yeah, cider and black for me. Sand, have a drink with me."

"Mocha?" Tanya asked.

Sandy nodded reluctantly.

"The thing is, I know how amazing she is, Sand. I know what it's like to lose her."

"You know what she was like as a teenager. Like you said, things change."

Bomber nodded. "I know that, alright? That's my whole point. It's not about pretending to listen in class anymore, it's all serious now."

"Are you in trouble, Tommy?"

The use of his real name made the colour drain from his face. "Nah, course not."

"I don't believe you." Sandy said.

He shrugged, maintaining eye contact.

"You just happened to be at a point in your life where you could drop everything and come back here to try and woo Cass?"

"She's that important to me." Bomber explained. "And you, Sand. I wanted to lay the old ghosts to rest."

"How do you plan on doing that?"

"Well, I need to wear you down and show you I'm not bad news."

"You were never bad news." Sandy admitted. "You just

made a stupid mistake. But you know what they say, fool me once shame on you, fool me twice shame on me."

"Yeah." Bomber said with a sigh. "I don't blame you. But you can't blame me for trying. I don't know if me and Cass could have a chance, but I'd like to find out. And I'd like to sit on the swings with you again some day, see who can reach the sky first."

Sandy let out a small laugh. "You remember that?"

"Course I do." He said with a smile, and Sandy couldn't help but return it. Even as a friend, even as a friend she had never been attracted to (despite all of the girls in Year 11 fancying him), a friend she had never coveted as more than a friend, even as a friend, to be under his spell, his attention, it was captivating. Addictive.

To her surprise, Sandy reached her arm out across the table and held out her hand for him to shake. "Here's to a second chance... as long as you're completely honest with both of us this time."

Bomber grinned, a natural, unrehearsed grin that made his eyes sparkle. He pretended to spit on his hand and then clasped his hand in hers, shaking up and down, up and down, until Tanya appeared with drinks.

"So, my old buddy, what have I missed?" Bomber asked, and the opportunity to be the recipient of that gaze for a while longer was too tempting to refuse.

Sandy told him everything.

How rocky things had been for a time at Books and Bakes, how well business was going now, how proud she was of Cass for beginning LA Nails, how proud she was of Cass for taking in Olivia. She told him how much she still missed her parents, how Coral was a liability in the kitchen at work but a magician on the till. She told him about The Cat, probably in too much detail, but he remained intent, laughing at the right places and cooing over the photographs she showed him on her phone. She told him about how the weather never improved in Waterfell Tweed and how she really must book a summer holiday in the sun. She told him random, unconnected pieces of news from the last decade, helping him remember who some of the people involved were - *you know, she used to have a Yorkshire Terrier and always had that purple stripe in her hair!*

When she realised the sky outside had grown dark, she grew self-conscious and apologised for talking at him for so long.

Bomber laughed it off. "I've missed your yacking!"

"And you?" Sandy asked, high with the thrill of catching up, bonding again. Eager to sit back and listen to his own long-winded, rambling, nonsensical update. "Tell me everything!"

Bomber shifted in his sheet and let out a small cough. "Just the normal, you know. Nothing much to tell. Great to catch up, though. I'd better get going."

And with that, he stood and left.

Sandy felt the bottom fall out of her stomach, an empty sensation taking over her body.

He'd done it again.

Sucked her in. Entranced her.

She shook her head, annoyed with herself more than him.

"These all done?" Tanya asked, collecting the empty pint glass and half-empty, cold, mug of mocha that Sandy had been too busy talking to drink.

"Yeah... thanks, Tanya."

"He's a bit of alright." Tanya said. "He's been around a bit last few days. Friend?"

"I wouldn't say that." Sandy said. "And he's bad news. Don't get any ideas."

"Oh." Tanya said, giving a conspirational wink. "Thanks for the heads up."

"Actually, I wanted to ask something but Tom's not around is he? Did Gurdip come in the night before he was killed?"

"He did." Tanya said. "I was on my own - Tom had gone to some meeting for all the local publicans. Rushed off my feet, I was."

"I see." Sandy said, relieved that Tom hadn't kept the information from her.

At least there was one man in her life she could trust.

9

"Ugh, I hope you've got some paracetamol in here." Coral moaned as she rummaged through Sandy's handbag.

The noise in Books and Bakes was raucous, fueled by children who had waited quite long enough and weren't happy about it.

Sandy glanced at her watch again.

"She should just tell you if she can't fit this into her busy schedule any more." Coral said, voicing Sandy's own thoughts with a little less tact.

"It's so unlike her though, she's usually bang on time." Sandy said.

It was clear that Penelope Harlow was not coming.

"Fancy doing it?" Sandy asked Coral, who winced at the idea.

"What are my options here?"

"Well, if I do it, you'll have to manage all the drinks on your own."

"Ugh." Coral moaned. "I've got a better chance of surviving down there with the kids. Fine. But I don't want to do this regularly Sandy, so speak to Penelope and find out what's happening."

"I will." Sandy promised. "And thank you."

"Right, boys and girls! It's a treat today, you've got me!" Coral announced as she removed her apron and walked through the seating area to the back of the cafe, where bean bags had been spread around. A group of hyperactive children bounced around from bean bag to bean bag, until Coral shushed them all and allowed them to choose from two books.

The story time group was a huge draw for Books and Bakes, attracting lots of the villagers but also people from neighbouring villages, where the meagre facilities on offer all closed down over the weekend. The children were amused while the parents without fail ordered drinks and cakes to enjoy.

"She not turned up again?" Bernice asked, poking her head out from the kitchen at the sound of Coral's voice leading the group.

Sandy shook her head.

"I hope everything's okay." Bernice said, eyebrows furrowed.

"Me too." Sandy said.

**

Sandy locked up on time, pulling her yellow mac on and braving the elements. There was a bitter wind howling through the village, and she pulled the zipper up to her chin and pulled the hood up over her head, then crossed the village square and walked past the little church.

She wondered how Olivia was doing in her work there and scolded herself for not sending her a good luck card.

After the church, she cut up the path that led into the grounds of Waterfell Manor, the stately home where Penelope and Benedict Harlow lived with their son Sebastian. The grounds were open to the public, and were a favourite choice of visiting walkers as well as the locals, who all carried a deep curiosity about the lives of the other half, the wealthy aristocrats who lived in the Manor.

The Harlow family were as down to earth as anyone living in an inherited 100-acre stately home could be, and Sandy wasn't surprised to see Benedict himself out walking, head protected under a deerstalker hat.

"Hallo, Sandy!" He called into the wind, his face red from the elements.

"Benedict, nice day for it." Sandy replied, having to shout to make herself heard. "No Penelope today?"

"Indoors making game pie, Lord have mercy!" Benedict called, or at least that's what it sounded like. The Harlows had staff, including a cook, so Sandy wondered if she had misheard. "Hoping if I get lost out here, dinner will be in the dog as they say!"

Sandy laughed. Benedict was charming. Self-aware enough to recognise how people may view him, humble enough to win over even the deepest skeptics with his complete devotion to Waterfell Tweed and interest in all of its inhabitants.

Years before, he had chanced upon a villager in the pub, who had, after a few too many pints, loudly interrogated Benedict about his wealth and the unfairness of it all. The man's car had just been written off, and he didn't have money to repair it, meaning he would have to cycle the 22 miles to work every day and night for the foreseeable future.

Benedict had listened patiently to the man's rant, shaking his head at the then-landlord's offer to intervene and throw the drunk out.

"No car, you say? Well, take mine, old boy." Benedict had said when the man paused for a sip of his ale, and handed across the keys to his own Range Rover.

The villager had used the car for months, until he had saved enough for his own to be repaired, and had returned it to Benedict in better condition than he'd received it in, transformed into the man's biggest fan.

Sandy smiled at the memory.

"Fancy joining us?" Benedict asked now, and Sandy wondered how tiring it must be, to be switched on, serving a public (even just a local public) constantly. Although, she then corrected herself, she didn't truly believe that Benedict saw it that way at all. Shame on her.

"I can't tonight, but thank you." Sandy said. "Give Penelope my love."

"Shall do." Benedict said, making a mock salute as if receiving orders. He strode on, heading back up the hill towards the big house.

He seemed to have absolutely no idea that Penelope had failed to attend the story time session. How curious.

**

Cass opened the door after a few seconds, her hair stacked on top of her head in a beehive, cheeks contoured. Her eyebrows were only part hair, others tattooed on, and her lips looked fuller than they had the week before.

"Wow." Sandy said as she walked in. "Look at you. Are you going out?"

"Oh no!" Cass said with a laugh, instinctively reaching for her face and placing a finger on her inflated lips. "Not been in from work long. Have to look the part."

"She's making an extra effort since Bomber's in town." Olivia called. She was lying on the settee, a bowl of popcorn balanced on her slim stomach, the remote control in her hand.

"I am not!" Cass exclaimed, but her cheeks flushed, even through her make-up.

"How's work going?" Sandy asked Olivia, wanting to avoid the subject of Bomber.

Olivia gave a dramatic groan. "It's exhausting."

"Really? What's he got you doing over there?"

Cass rolled her eyes. "She's just not used to hard work."

"Don't listen to her, Auntie Sandy. I'm at school all day, then at work, it's really hard. I am enjoying it, though."

"Well, that's good. Make sure you're keeping up with your schoolwork though, okay?"

"On that note, you've got homework, remember." Cass said, then looked at Sandy. "Drink?"

"I'm okay thanks, I just wanted to pop in and see the working girl."

"Well, you've seen her. She's here all week, glued to the settee as you can see."

"I'm exhausted!" Olivia repeated.

Sandy smiled at their interaction.

Cass handed her a mug of mocha, which Sandy accepted with amusement. "Erm, thanks, I think I said no though? And I've got to ask, are your lips new?"

Cass beamed, the smile transforming her face. "Do ya like them? They're not too big, are they?"

Sandy inspected her friend's face. The plump lips were subtle, perhaps, but Sandy knew that face so well, knew what it looked like naturally beneath the make-up and beauty treatments. "No, they're not too big. What have you done, though? Is that botox?"

"No!" Cass exclaimed, using the same high-pitched tone she had used with Sandy when they were teenagers and Sandy had thought that eyeliner was lipliner for goths. "It's just a little filler. I went to a beauty show the other day and they'd got all these treatments you could try. I've always fancied giving my lips a bit more, ya know, oomph. Mine are so pathetic."

"You've got lovely lips." Sandy insisted, although she knew that out of the two of them her own lips had the better natural shape, the bee-stung look that her friend had always envied. Out of all of her face, her lips were probably the most neglected area. She never wore lipstick. In fact, the only time she applied anything to her lips was in the thick of winter when they grew chapped and sore. Then she'd apply a chapstick throughout the day hungrily, desperate for some moisture to seep in and soothe the pain. When they healed, she promptly forgot all about her lips for another 12 months, whereas Cass had a drawer just for lipsticks, mountains of them that all looked the same colour, and a smaller mountain of bright and garish colours.

In fact, Sandy realised, there was every chance she had noticed her friend's lips tonight because they were bare, not because they were any larger. She wouldn't tell Cass that.

"How's the investigation coming along? I heard everyone thinks it's some mad old farmer."

"Victor Dent. Know him?" Sandy asked.

"Oh, yeah, I'm always hanging out with the farmers." Cass said with a wink.

Sandy laughed. "I met him, he's pretty protective of his land."

"No crime in that, surely?" Cass said.

"I need to know more." Sandy said, the cogs in her mind turning as she took a sip of the mocha she hadn't wanted until she'd seen, and smelt, it. "And then I've got Penelope acting all strange."

"Strange? How?"

"She didn't turn up for story time again today."

"That is strange." Cass admitted. Some people were scatty, unreliable, but the Harlows took their commitments to Waterfell Tweed seriously. It wasn't a light agreement to Penelope, or at least Sandy hadn't considered it to be until recently.

"I know. I'm worried about her."

"Oh, don't be, she'll be fine. You know Penelope, stiff upper lip and all that."

Sandy smiled, but the unease in her stomach didn't settle.

"You're due your next eyebrow appointment, you know." Cass said, with a pointed look.

"They're still tidy." Sandy objected. She was in no rush to put herself through the pain of waxing again.

"That's the time to get it done, before they're out of control." Cass explained with a grin. Her own eyebrows never had a single hair out of place. She knew that Cass plucked them daily, looking in the mirror each morning and pulling out any single hairs that weren't quite where they should be. Sandy shuddered at the thought of putting herself through that pain each day. "Pop in tomorrow, I'll fit you in."

"Can I have mine done too?" Olivia called from the settee.

"Noooooo." Cass drawled. "I've already told you, you're too young."

Olivia sighed and pushed her body off the settee, walking over to join them. "I'll go and do my homework then since I'm just a kid."

"Okay." Cass said with a smile, amused by Olivia's attempt at being a stroppy teenager.

Olivia planted a kiss on Sandy's cheek and left them to it, taking the stairs two at a time to her bedroom.

"Sit?" Cass suggested now the settee was empty.

"I'm gonna get going, but thanks for the drink. There's something I need to do before it gets dark."

Cass pulled her in for a hug but didn't ask where she was going. Her mind, just like her hair and her new lips, was distracted by something. And Sandy knew exactly who that was.

10

"*I*f I die tonight, don't be mad at me." Sandy whispered. "You know what I'm like, I just can't keep my nose out. And I've got a hunch. So, please don't be too mad. I love you."

She hung up the phone, knowing how furious Tom would be when he heard the voicemail, and tucked it into the pocket of her yellow mac.

It was a clear evening, the sun still high in the sky, and the quiet was serene. As Sandy got out of the car, closing her door with as much force as she could to signal her arrival, she was struck by the silence, interrupted only by the bleating of sheep, a secret conversation from ewe to ewe, about her perhaps. Raising the alarm. Although the sheep seemed far too interested in their grazing to be concerned by her.

The ledge stood ahead of her, Black Rock, not a kissing couple in sight. Transformed from a spot to visit in secret, to a place to avoid.

Sandy wasn't heading there tonight, though.

She climbed the sty and followed the public footpath,

the ground firm and solid beneath her, recovered from the storm.

The farmhouse stood ahead of her, off the path of course, and she tried to walk with a stomp, to cough regularly, to do all she could to allow Victor Dent to hear her coming. She had a feeling that if her presence was announced by a knock on his door, it would be very bad for her.

Her stomach flipped as she walked, focused on one step in front of the other, heartbeat pounding in her ears.

The old man scared her, which was not surprising as that was his intention.

It was madness to visit him, alone.

To not tell anyone where she was going.

She thought that Tom might guess, from her voicemail, but he was on shift at The Tweed and wouldn't check his phone until after he'd locked up. That was hours away.

Sandy wondered whether to turn and walk away, to return another day with back-up, or to forget the whole thing entirely.

But then she remembered Anastasia's devastation, her certainty that Gurdip hadn't fallen.

Nobody else was helping the widow.

It was down to Sandy.

She marched onward, leaving the path and traipsing through the long grass, almost stumbling twice in unseen dips and holes, until she reached the farmhouse, a sturdy stone building with single-pane windows, and a stream of smoke puffing out of the chimney.

She tapped twice, loud enough to be heard but not loud enough to cause concern, and waited.

And waited.

She tapped again, more forcefully, and the door opened

with her touch, revealing a dark corridor lined with photographs. Dozens of photographs. Sandy tried not to look, surprised by their presence and understanding their significance. Victor Dent was not a man who would want her to scrutinise his photographs.

"Mr Dent?" She called, already telling herself that he was out, that he was a farmer who would be busy with his farm work, not sitting at home for her visit.

"In here!" A strangled voice came, and Sandy forgot her nerves and darted down the hallway, following the voice.

Victor Dent was sprawled on the floor in the kitchen, same moth-eaten jumper on, eyes swimming with pain.

"Oh my, it's me Mr Dent, Sandy, from the village. Are you okay?"

He attempted to sit up but groaned.

"Don't try to move, I'll call an ambulance. What happened?"

"Making a drink." He said, eyes darting to the work surface where a china cup filled with water and a teabag stood. "Didn't see the water had spilt, fell all my length."

"Okay. Let me get an ambulance."

"No, don't!" He protested. "They'll have Social Services all over this place. I don't want no-one questioning whether I can live alone."

"But if you can't move, Mr Dent..."

"Victor, for cripes sake. Am I really that ancient that I've stopped having a first name? Ere, hold my arm, I'll be 'rate now."

"I really think we should get some medical help." Sandy said.

Victor Dent glared at her, then, with sheer stubbornness, pushed himself to a sitting position, every movement forcing a gasp out of him.

"Okay?" Sandy asked. "Take it steady."

"Take it steady." He repeated, mocking. Sandy looked at him and thought that Cass would love to get her wax on his eyebrows. They were so long they almost met his eyelashes, as if his facial hair was creating a prison to trap his face in.

"Now, get my stick, over there." He pointed back down the hall, to the front door. Sandy saw it, a beautiful walking stick topped with a golden eagle. Over the banister hung a black suit jacket, covered in a thick layer of dust.

"Help me up." Victor commanded, and Sandy gripped under his arms, close enough to be surprised by the fresh soap scent from his body. Once standing, he clung to the walking stick with his right hand and Sandy held on to his left arm. "In here, this is where I live."

The back room was old-fashioned and dusty, the wallpaper thick and dark green, curtains to match. Sandy guided him to a high-backed chair, one chosen for practicality not appearance, and stood in front of him.

"Shall I finish that tea off for you?" She asked, amazed by the man's strength and wary of leaving him alone.

"Two sugars." He said, then flashed her a smile, revealing a perfect white set of dentures. "Get yourself one, lass."

Sandy didn't get herself one, mainly because of spotting what she was sure were mouse droppings on the kitchen counter. She picked a clean cup - china again, pink rose design - for Victor and gave it a thorough wash with hot water. She couldn't see washing up liquid and didn't want to go through his cupboards more than she needed to.

"Here you go, tea with two sugars. That'll do you good. How are you feeling now, where does it hurt?"

He erupted into a mix of a laugh and a coughing fit.

"Where does it hurt? That's a good one. Hurts everywhere, has done for years."

"Are you sure you don't want -"

"I've already told you, no."

"Okay." Sandy said. "Well, I'd like to stay for a bit and just keep an eye on you, would that be ok?"

To her surprise, he shrugged indifference.

"It's a lovely big farmhouse."

"Too big." He moaned. "But I'll not leave."

"Do you find it hard looking after it all?"

"I'm not here, am I?" He asked. "I'm out there. This place is just to rest my head, have a cup of tea but I can't even do that right."

"We all have accidents." Sandy said with a weak smile. She heard the condescending tone of her own voice, as if she were talking to a small child who had just wet their big girl pants.

"What were you doing out here anyway?"

"I came to see you." Sandy admitted. "Glad I did, now."

"Hmm... what do you want to come and see an old man like me for?"

"You sounded really angry the other night."

He looked at her blankly.

"Do you remember? You came out to me and my, erm, Tom. We were at Black Rock."

Victor Dent rolled his eyes. "No, I don't remember you. I go out to twenty people a day on there!"

"Why does it bother you so much, them being there?" Sandy asked.

"Is that what you came to ask me?" Victor asked, holding her gaze, his mouth stern, thin lines, downturned.

"Yeah, I guess it is."

Victor sighed, lost in his thoughts. He reached across to

the coffee table next to his chair and picked up a photo frame. Gazed at it, a smile creeping across his face, then held it out to Sandy.

It was old, the photograph dated by it's low resolution. In it, a young man stood atop Black Rock, a border collie by his side, a grin on his face.

"Travis." Victor said, the word costing him something visceral.

"Travis? He looks happy."

"He was."

Sandy looked up at him, encouraging him to continue. To speak, to share the pain that she suspected he had hidden for years.

"My son." Victor croaked, tears escaping him. He wiped them away with a furious, shaky hand. "Black Rock's his."

"You're protecting the land for him." Sandy said.

He nodded. "He was only 26. No age. No age at all."

"What happened to him, Victor?" Sandy asked.

"Nobody can tell us." He admitted, and began to weep, his cry soft and quiet, desperate. "They found his body, at least. We got to bury him. But they can't say what happened."

"I'm so sorry." Sandy said, feeling herself choke up. Her heart broke for Victor Dent, for the questions he had that wouldn't be answered, the son he wouldn't see grow to inherit Black Rock, and the return each night to this ramshackle house filled with memories.

"Twenty years since I heard his voice." Victor said.

Sandy reached across the space between them and held the old man's hand in hers.

"That's why you don't want people on Black Rock. Why not just tell them that, Victor? People would understand."

He shook his head violently. "People don't need to know my business. I can't use his name like that, as if it's gossip."

"People think you killed Gurdip."

The words startled him. "Me? Kill someone?"

"I don't think you did it, Victor, but that's the reputation you're building by being so angry. People are scared of you."

Victor reached back to the coffee table and handed Sandy another photo frame, this one clearly showing Victor himself as the proud groom, standing next to a beautiful bride.

"She left because she was scared, too." Victor admitted. "Valerie. We tried to hold it together, but you can't lose a child and hold it together. She turned to God, I turned to hate. When she left, I was glad. All I wanted was my boy, not that stupid woman with her Bibles and her praying for everyone and everything. As if anyone needed more prayers than our boy. And then she left, scared I'd hit her the next time. Who knows, maybe I would. Maybe people should be scared."

"I'm not scared." Sandy said, the honesty of the words surprising her. "I think you've been through something awful, and you've hidden yourself away when there's a whole village ready to support you."

"Nah, my bridges are burnt down there."

Sandy smiled and shook her head. "You've got one fan left at least."

He looked at her, head cocked to one side.

"Dorie." Sandy explained. "She won't hear a bad word about you."

"Ah... yes. A loss sends most people running, you know. They come to the funeral but then they think life carries on, and it doesn't. Dorie was good, good to Valerie. She knew loss, she knew it didn't go away after the funeral."

Sandy nodded. Grief. The common thread creating the most unexpected relationships.

"How is she? Haven't seen her in years."

"She's good." Sandy said. "Dealing with her loneliness in her own way, I think. Being around people helps her."

"Nothing subtle about you, is there?" Victor said with a laugh.

Sandy flushed but grinned. "I own the cafe in the village. I'd really like you to come in, when you're feeling better. And I promise you a warm welcome."

Victor considered the request and nodded, slowly.

"I think maybe it's time you stopped isolating yourself. I'm sure your son wouldn't want that to be your life."

Victor began to cry again at the mention of Travis.

"I liked Gurdip." He said. "He was alright. He'd come and knock me up sometimes, see how I was. I know about losing someone, lass, there's no way I'd put another person through that. Unless…"

Sandy watched him, saw the softness disappear from his eyes.

"Unless they can tell me who took my boy. Then I'd do it. So, no, I didn't kill Gurdip. I'm saving myself. Saving myself for someone who deserves it. It's been a long time coming."

Sandy swallowed and nodded her head.

It was a pointless argument, and one she might not want to have in any event.

If Victor did find out who had killed his son, could she blame him for wanting to exact revenge?

Surely, even his religious wife wouldn't criticise him. Didn't the Bible itself advise: *an eye for an eye*?

**

Sandy settled Victor for the night, him ferociously refusing her suggestion that she help him upstairs to bed.

She glanced at the photographs in the hall on her way out.

Every single one showing the boy he had loved and lost.

She trudged back through the grass, along the footpath, and towards Black Rock, where she allowed herself to stand for a moment, imagining the future Victor had planned.

She began to cry and looked down as she saw something caught under a stone near her feet.

She bent down and pulled at the soft piece of fabric, dirtied by the elements.

A handkerchief.

She clasped it in her hand, her fingers rubbing away at the dirt, until a pattern was revealed in one corner.

A swirl, no not a pattern, but writing.

Letters.

The handkerchief, obviously well-made, fine quality and craftsmanship, embossed in the corner:

PH

11

*S*andy had refused the offers from friends to attend the funeral together, knowing that she wouldn't have time to stand in the church and pay her final respects and have the food prepared in time for the wake.

Bernice had insisted that she also skip the service to help, even though it fell on a day she wouldn't usually work, and Sandy had been relieved.

"It's all going to work fine." Bernice reassured her as they retreated to the back of Books and Bakes, leaving Coral and Derrick to manage the front of house.

The kitchen had been transformed to a treasure trove of fresh food. The counters were stacked high with plump, red tomatoes, large spring onions, fresh gem lettuce, cucumbers bigger than Sandy had ever seen before.

She'd visited the farm shop on the outskirts of the village, paying their inflated prices for their hand-reared produce, and had asked Anastasia for potatoes out of her own garden, and the potato salad recipe. The request had made the woman weep again, fiddling with the gold cross around her neck as she abandoned her half-dragged cigarette in an ashtray on the dining table.

She didn't know the recipe, she'd confessed. It was Gurdip's not hers. She thought it was mayonnaise with a little mustard, chopped spring onions, maybe chives too. Lots of sea salt and black pepper.

The potato salad would be the focal point of the buffet, and Sandy was left trying to recreate a dead man's recipe. The thought made her insides churn.

"Come on, no time to flap now." Bernice commanded, and Sandy was once again grateful for her no-nonsense attitude. "The potatoes need to be getting on, you want to chop?"

"Yes, captain." Sandy teased, but she was happy to follow orders. Bernice was much better at following through with a well-organised plan than she was.

"Okay. So, we'll have the potato salad, the quiches'll be done in a minute so they'll cool nicely, I'll make us a nice salad."

"Thanks, B." Sandy said as she pulled a knife out of a drawer. She placed it down on the cutting board then washed her hands, enjoying the meditative routine of it. She was always careful to wash the length of each finger as well as the spots in between.

"How's Anastasia doing?" Bernice asked as she chopped lengths of gem lettuce and tossed them into a large salad bowl.

"As you'd expect." Sandy said. "I worry for her because I don't know who she knows really, who she's got to talk to and stuff."

"She might not be a talker."

"True." Sandy said with a nod. She fell into a rhythm as

she chopped the potatoes into two chunks each, dropping the pieces into a large pan.

"These tomatoes smell amazing." Bernice gushed, holding a tomato under Sandy's nose. She sniffed obediently.

"You get what you pay for." Sandy said with a laugh, although the smell was glorious. It was the smell of one more bounce on the trampoline before bed, the smell of spending all day in the garden in a swimming costume while her mother tried to concentrate on reading a book, hidden beneath enormous sunglasses that scared Sandy, in case her mum stopped being her mum when her eyes were hidden. "Smells like childhood."

"Closest we'll get now." Bernice said, returning her attention to the chopping.

"Would you like to go back in time to your childhood?" Sandy asked as she poured boiling water into the pan and turned on the gas, adding a sprinkle of sea salt to the water.

"Nah." Bernice said. "I think I prefer being the grown up. I was never too good at being a carefree kid."

"That doesn't surprise me." Sandy admitted. "I'd love to be a kid again, just for a bit. The days were so endless then, weren't they? Everything seemed bigger."

Bernice glanced around at her. "Set a timer on those potatoes."

Sandy set the timer and, when she was sure Bernice wasn't watching, rolled her eyes, enjoying the feeling of being a naughty child once more.

**

The Tweed was full of mourners.

It felt as though the whole of the village had turned out to say farewell to Gurdip, all dressed in their darkest colours, faces sombre until they spotted the food and exclaimed over it.

Sandy had typed a note explaining that the fresh buffet was inspired by Gurdip's love of fresh, homegrown produce, and ending with an invitation for the mourners to pick up a plate, tuck in, and join Anastasia in enjoying this meal in Gurdip's memory.

Several mourners became watery-eyed when they read the note.

Dorie Slaughter read it first, of course, and let out a small, strangled cry, before composing herself. She nodded her head repeatedly as she piled her plate high with the natural feast, then caught Sandy's eye. The connection caused a single tear to drip down her cheek, and Sandy wondered how much of her sorrow was for Gurdip, and how much was the memory of losing her own husband years before.

Felix Bartholomew, dressed as smart as he was on any other day, followed Dorie and took a seat beside her. Sandy watched as he clasped his hand in hers and gave her a reassuring smile, even as his own lips wobbled. Watching the two, both widowed, made Sandy's heart smile and break at the same time.

"A good man." Benedict Harlow murmured as he worked his way down the food tables with his wife and son by his side. "A good man, indeed, and what a wonderful feast in his honour."

"Good job, Sandy." Sebastian said with a wink. The young man's constant flirting was harmless and she shook her head in his direction with a smile.

"The famous potato salad." Benedict exclaimed as his wife dabbed at her eyes with a silk handkerchief. "Let's give it a whirl."

Sandy glanced at Bernice.

"Where's Anastasia?" She asked.

Bernice shrugged. "I haven't seen her yet."

"Hmm, I hope she's okay."

"She might just need a minute to compose herself."

"Yeah, maybe." Sandy said doubtfully. Anastasia had been so keen to see the food, to ensure it was right, it was strange that she wasn't present.

"She'll come." Bernice said.

But she didn't.

Sandy watched the clock as more and more mourners tucked into their first, and then second, helpings. Compliments poured in for her and Bernice, for the freshness of the food, the vibrant taste of the tomatoes and the almost-angry bite of the radishes, compared with the sweetness of the warm corn on the cob pieces, each one adorned with a sliver of butter and then wrapped in foil to retain heat.

"Maybe I'll become a vegetarian after all?" Gus Sanders, the butcher, declared noisily after a full second plate of food and several pints of beer. His wife, Poppy, rolled her eyes and told him to be quiet, which seemed to be her role at most wakes.

Tom worked the bar throughout the wake, and occasionally Sandy would glance his way and watch him work. She liked to see him lost in the pouring of a pint, or the listening to a story from a patron that he'd probably already heard and wasn't interested in. One time, as he handed several coins of change to Benedict Harlow, he looked up and saw her watching him. His cheeks flushed a delicious shape of pink, salmon really, and Sandy had to bite her lip to stop her laughing out loud at how adorable he looked.

"There's gonna be no food left for her." Sandy said, later, as the platters cleared.

"She'll come." Bernice insisted.

But she didn't.

Derrick, who had come straight to the wake after finishing his shift at work, raised a toast to Gurdip, to the man who had helped him when he was homeless, who had shown him kindness when many others hadn't.

The whole of the pub raised their glass and agreed that Gurdip was a fine man.

"Taken too soon." Derrick said, his glass held high.

"Taken too soon." The whole of the pub repeated in unison, causing a shiver to travel down Sandy's spine.

Gradually, the crowd thinned out, and reluctantly Sandy began to clear the remaining food into plastic storage tubs. The food had been a success. Nobody had queried why the usual buffet choices weren't present, and the fresh food had certainly looked more bright and colourful.

"Night, Sandy." Derrick called on his way out. Sandy waved in his direction.

It was growing dark outside.

The wake, and the part of the event that Sandy always thought of as the after-wake, for the committed mourners or the committed drinkers, had lasted hours.

She collected the tubs of remaining food in a fabric shopper bag from her handbag and turned to see Bernice emerge from the ladies.

"Can you finish up here?" Sandy asked.

Bernice smiled. "Of course. I wondered when you'd go to her."

**

It was easy to pick out Gurdip's house because every single light was on.

A half-full tip took up the road in front of the house.

Sandy knocked on the door, then again, and then again, until eventually Anastasia answered. Her hair was scooped up into a high, messy bun, and she wore an oversized t-shirt, grey with a cartoon man on, the caption reading "YOU'RE LOOKING AT A FUTURE DOCTOR". The t-shirt fell almost down to her knees, her legs were bare.

"Sandy?" She rasped. "Do I owe you some more money?"

"Oh, God, no." Sandy said, her cheeks flaming. "No, I just wanted to check on you. I brought the leftovers. Can I come in?"

Anastasia held the door open, and the sight caused Sandy to take a breath.

"Wow, this is different."

The hallway was transformed. A new radiator sat, white and perfect, on the wall, surrounded by freshly painted cream walls. The stench of the fumes was heavy in the air, not unpleasant, compared to the thick nicotine it had replaced.

"Buyers want neutral, apparently." Anastasia said with a shrug.

"Buyers?" Sandy repeated.

Anastasia nodded. "I can't stay here. There's too much I want to say and nobody to listen."

"There's a lot of support for you here, honestly. The wake was jam-packed."

Anastasia sighed. "People are sad that Gurdip died, but

they're not my friends. I need to get back to the people who love me."

Sandy nodded. "I can understand that. But the house might not sell quickly. Don't be a stranger, hey, while you're still here."

"You don't want to get to know me, okay?"

"Okay." Sandy said, having no intention of arguing with a widow on the day of her husband's funeral. "I just wanted to see if you were okay, that's all."

"But you don't. Not really." Anastasia said. "People are full of those stupid platitudes, but nobody can help it if you admit that, actually, you're not okay, and you'll never be okay again. Because that's how I feel, okay? If you really want to know... geeze... what am I doing? Just go, Sandy. Thank you for the wake. I appreciate it, but it doesn't make us friends."

Sandy held Anastasia's gaze, before nodding and seeing herself out of the property.

Anastasia was right.

They weren't friends.

12

The Cat met her at the front door, waiting on the mat when she opened the door.

"Oh, you're adorable!" Sandy exclaimed. She closed the door behind her and sat right there, on the bristly mat, and The Cat padded across to her and curled up on her lap, a contented purr escaping from him as he drifted to sleep.

Sandy remained in that position, enjoying the warmth his body produced, until a knock at the front door disturbed them both.

The Cat jumped up and gave her a disdainful look, as if she had personally arranged the knock to disrupt his evening.

She climbed to her feet and opened the door.

"Surprise!" Cass called, a grin on her plumped-up lips and a bottle of white wine in her hand. "Are you alone? Can I come in?"

"You're interrupting amazing cuddles actually..."

"Oh." Cass said, dejected.

"With The Cat. Course you can come in." Sandy said, holding the door open for her friend, who saw her own way through to the kitchen and pulled two glasses out of the cupboard. "No wine for me, been a rough day."

"They're the days that need wine." Cass said. "Shall I pop the kettle on?"

"Nah, I'm fine. Sort yourself, though."

"Oh, I am!" Cass said, already returning down the hallway with a full glass of wine in her hand. She walked past Sandy and plopped herself down on the settee. "So, rough day how?"

"Gurdip's wake."

"Oh! How was the potato salad?"

"People seemed to like it, and Anastasia never turned up, so if it didn't taste like Gurdip's, nobody will ever know..."

"Result." Cass said.

"Hmm." Sandy murmured.

"Oh come on, Sand. That's the end of your involvement. Don't make everyone else's problems yours."

"Is that what I'm doing?" Sandy asked, a challenge in her tone. No longer talking about Gurdip.

"Well... it should be my choice whether I forgive Bomber."

Sandy sighed. "Of course it should. I do know that, you know. But I can't stop wanting to protect you. I don't turn that on and off like he does."

"Ouch." Cass exclaimed, clutching her chest as if Sandy's words had shot her.

Sandy rolled her eyes.

"If I get hurt again, are you going to still be there?"

"Of course I am." Sandy said. "You don't need to ask."

"And will you say, I told you so?"

"Yeah, I probably will say that." Sandy admitted. "But I'll wipe your tears as well. And buy you the really good chocolate ice cream."

"That solves everything." Cass said with an easy laugh.

"That's a deal then." Sandy said. "Is there anything I should know?"

"He's been hiding something."

"I knew it." Sandy said. "Is it about Gurdip? I know he's lying about the day he arrived here."

"Please..."

"Okay." Sandy said. "Go on, I'll listen."

"He wanted to tell you himself. He said you were chatting in The Tweed the other night, but he lost his nerve."

"Did he hurt him?" Sandy asked, then clasped a hand over her mouth. "Sorry. I'll listen."

"He's penniless." Cass said after a thirsty gulp of the wine. She laughed and shrugged. "He had a business, well a few actually, but he's lost everything."

"That's it?" Sandy asked.

"That's it." Cass said. "I've grilled him so hard, Sand... and I've told him, I don't even want to see his face as a friend if I can't trust him. One lie, and it's done. And, I believe him."

"Well, he has been pretty vague about his life since he came back."

"I know, this is why. He's thought the less he said, he wouldn't have to actually lie about it. And he didn't want to be a new face arriving in the village on the day someone died, not when you were sniffing around it being a murder."

"That makes sense." Sandy accepted. "What are his plans, then?"

"He doesn't know. He's staying with relatives nearby for a bit, and he needs work. I'm not solving his problems for him."

"What are his plans with you?"

Cass shrugged. "We're just getting to know each other

again. Maybe it'll lead somewhere, I don't know. The money stuff, that doesn't bother me. I'm doing fine on my own anyway, it's not like I need his money, but I've got Olivia to look after, I don't want to take on someone else to look after."

"No way." Sandy agreed. "He's a grown man, he needs to help himself. There's work out there."

"He's doing some labouring, he's got old school contacts and they're sending him a few days here and there. He'll be fine, I keep telling him that. We've both had our hard times and come through, haven't we?"

Sandy smiled. "I wish he'd just told me. He left me in the pub that night feeling like a complete moron. I'd just opened up to him about my life and he got up and left."

"He told me. And I told him I wouldn't be keeping any secrets from you." Cass said. "That made him laugh. We still come as a pair, you know."

"Of course." Sandy said with a grin.

"I need to say something..." Cass said, her voice serious. "I've not been very supportive about you and Tom. I'm sorry. I've just been scared of losing you, scared you might not have time for me any more."

"Oh you daft sod." Sandy said. She scooted across the settee and pulled Cass in for a hug, the glass of wine sloshing over the rim and wetting both of their tops. "I'll always have time for you."

"Well, I want you to know I'm happy for you. And I like Tom. He's a good guy. So, if things with you are getting more serious, don't back off for my sake."

Sandy pulled her friend in closer, overcome with emotion, because that's exactly what she had been doing. Keeping Tom at arm's length at times, limiting the size of the role he played in her life. Acting, and thinking, like a single woman instead of a woman with an exciting new relationship and a man who, apparently, thought the world of her.

She had wondered at times if she was not ready for the relationship. She had felt the conflicting feelings of loving watching Tom across a room, but not wanting him to cross the room and speak to her. Her phone still listed her emergency contact as Cass, even though she knew Tom had had to update his medical information and had listed her as his next of kin; a move that had caused her stomach to flip with a mixture of emotions she couldn't even begin to name.

But, she realised, it wasn't fear for herself.

It was fear of alienating her best friend.

And with Cass' blessing, a weight was lifted from her shoulders.

"For what it's worth." Sandy said, taking a deep breath to buy time to formulate her thoughts. "If you have got a second chance at love with Bomber, I think you should take it. Try it, at least."

"You're getting all sentimental in your old age." Cass teased.

"Anastasia's leaving." Sandy blurted out, as she pulled the old tartan blanket from the back of the settee and spread it over her and Cass' laps.

"No surprise really."

"No, I guess. It made me think how heartbreaking it must be to lose the man you love."

"Well, yeah." Cass said. "And this place would only be a reminder for her."

"Why wouldn't she want the reminder?" Sandy asked.

Cass shrugged. "People deal with grief in different ways. With her thinking it wasn't an accident, sounds like she's in shock about the whole thing."

"I went back to Black Rock, you know. I found something."

Cass' eyes widened.

"Penelope Harlow's handkerchief."

"And? You think she's got something to do with it?"

"I don't know." Sandy admitted. "I wouldn't it that was all it was, but she's been acting strange recently. She's unreliable at story time, and she was strange at the wake today. It just seems a bit off."

"Is there even any evidence to suggest it wasn't an accident, though?"

Sandy shrugged. "It doesn't add up, him falling in such a well-known place, so near the road. It wasn't his land, he wasn't out with his sheep so he must have chosen to go to Black Rock."

"Another woman." Cass said.

"I don't want to think that." Sandy said. "Imagine breaking that news to Anastasia."

"It's the obvious reason he'd be on someone else's land, though. Somewhere where Anastasia wouldn't go to look for him."

"I don't know if he was the sort to be unfaithful. It seems they were a pretty strong couple."

"Oh, come on." Cass said, taking a slurp of wine and then wiping her mouth with the back of her hand. "Nobody knows what goes on in a relationship, not really."

"She followed him here so he could follow his dreams."

"Or they ran away to escape something."

"You're so cynical." Sandy admonished, but her friend's words struck a chord with her.

"Let's say he did have an affair, and Anastasia pushed for the fresh start here, but maybe that other woman didn't want to give him up. Maybe he didn't want to give her up."

"It's possible I guess... but where does Penelope fit in?"

"Who says she does?" Cass asked, curling her long, slim legs underneath her on the settee. "Finding a handkerchief hardly proves she was there when Gurdip died. How do you even know its hers?"

"It's embossed. And I saw her with an identical one today, wiping fake tears from her eyes."

"Crocodile tears, nice."

Sandy sighed. "I need to ask her about it."

"Great plan." Cass said. "Somewhere quiet and remote, maybe with a high ledge?"

"Ha ha." Sandy retorted. "You're even more spunky than normal tonight, is this the effect Bomber has on you?"

Cass pulled a face, screwing her nose up so it crinkled and looked piggish. "I'm sleeping here tonight, by the way."

"What about Olivia?"

"She's having her first sleepover with some girl from school. Highly exciting. She packed enough for a week, honestly. Who knows when I'll see her again."

"She's settling in so well. You've done a brilliant job with her."

"Yeah, I'm proud of myself. I didn't expect to be raising a teenager, but I wouldn't change it now. It feels right."

"Is she still enjoying work?"

"Loving it." Cass said, her voice growing quiet as she settled herself into a foetal position, her head on a tartan cushion. "She's surprising herself with her confidence. Apparently, Rob Fields isn't the most organised of people. She's been setting up whole new filing systems, a new electronic calendar system that links with his phone straight away, all sorts really."

"She's a good kid." Sandy said.

"She is. I don't think she'll stay with me much longer, though."

"What do you mean?"

"As soon as she's old enough I think she'll be wanting to move in with Derrick."

"Really? Would you let her?"

"I couldn't stop her, could I? And he's besotted with her, I know he'd look after her. She's got this scrapbook under her bed, I found it the other night, and she's cutting out photos of furniture she likes, from the Argos catalogue you know? And there's recipes cut out from magazines and things like, how to change a lightbulb. So I know they're talking about it. Or it's in her mind. She's not actually mentioned it to me, though, so don't say anything to her."

"No, course not. That's so sweet, a scrapbook to help her prepare for it."

"I know, I was planning my dream wedding, nothing as practical as moving out."

Cass yawned then, her mouth stretched so wide open it looked unnatural, her dazzling white teeth shining out even in the dim light of the evening, and she closed her eyes and nestled her head deeper into the cushion. Within seconds, her breath settled into the steady, content rhythm of sleep, and Sandy draped the blanket over her and stood up, then crept out of the room.

She climbed the stairs and changed into her pyjamas, then got into her bed and typed out a text message.

Just thinking of you. I love you. x

13

*S*andy arrived early, earlier than it was polite to arrive unannounced at someone's home unless it was an emergency or a particularly close friend.

Sandy knew she couldn't pretend the second was true, and she wasn't sure that it was an emergency.

But she did know that the earlier the better.

The more chance her knock at the large, heavy door would be opened by Penelope herself, and not the staff.

She knocked lightly, not wanting to wake anyone, meaning Sebastian, who may still be asleep. To her surprise, the clip of heels approached the door immediately, and Penelope appeared, dressed in a black trouser suit with a snake print blouse beneath.

"Wow, you look great Penelope. Off somewhere nice?" Sandy said.

"I'm due in the city to see the accountants but the darn taxi hasn't arrived. I thought you were him."

"I could be." Sandy offered.

"Pardon?"

"I could take you where you need to get."

Penelope furrowed her eyebrows and looked at the expensive watch on her slender wrist. "Would you mind? I wouldn't ask but I really can't be late."

"Of course not, it's fine." Sandy said.

Penelope nodded and left the Manor without so much as a backwards glance. She followed Sandy across the gravel to her old Land Rover, a car that Sandy guessed Penelope would actually feel at home in.

She quickly cleared her sunglasses case and the mystery novel she was reading from the passenger side of the car to allow Penelope to sit down.

"Do you find much time to read?" Penelope asked, noticing the book that Sandy carefully placed on the back seat.

"Always." Sandy admitted. "Five minutes in traffic, ten minutes at lunch, a few pages at bed time. I'm always making time to read. Where are we going?"

"I'm getting the train from Buxton, could you run me to the station there?"

"Of course." Sandy said. She had nothing else to do so early in the morning, and the confined quarters of the car might help the conversation flow. "Headed to London?"

Penelope nodded. "Benedict usually does these things but he's dreadfully ill."

"Oh no. What's wrong?" Sandy asked, instinctively wondering if it could be food poisoning from her buffet. It was one of the problems of seeing her customers so regularly; whenever one of them commented on having had a sickness bug or a spate of diarrhoea (why such things were public conversations, Sandy would never understand), Sandy had a moment of queasiness while she calculated when the person had last ate her food.

"He came down with a migraine after the wake, awfully

sudden, and far too short notice to rearrange the meeting. So, here I am, off to do the job myself."

"Well, I hope it goes well." Sandy said.

"What were you knocking for? It's awfully early for a visit."

"I know, I'm sorry. I wanted to catch you on your own."

"Oh?" Penelope asked, an eyebrow raised.

"I'm worried about you." Sandy admitted. "You haven't seemed yourself for a while. You missed story time last week, and that's fine, if you're too busy or whatever I really would understand... but you haven't mentioned it since so it's like you don't..."

"Don't realise I missed it at all." Penelope said. "Quite."

"Is everything okay?"

Penelope let out a breath as she flexed her slender fingers. "No, Sandy, it's not."

Sandy nodded, gaze on the road, hoping her silence would encourage Penelope to continue talking.

"I don't know how but my spark for life has up and gone." Penelope said, her voice cheery, as if she was curious and entertained by the problem. "Some days, I don't even make it out of bed. Benedict says it's my age, that I'm enjoying some well-earnt rest, but I can't believe that. My life has hardly been one of physical labour, what have I done to earn a rest?"

"A lot's happened recently, though, with the..."

"The murders." Penelope finished. "Of course. And I'm sure this is a little slump that will disappear as soon as it arrived."

"It must be nice to have Sebastian home." Sandy said.

"You can't imagine the worry, Sandy. Knowing he was out in the other side of the world, hours away by plane if he needed us. Of course, it's not the same. He's come home a man. Won't even let me make him a hot cocoa at bed time any more. I loved that routine, always did it myself instead of asking the help."

"I used to love hot cocoa." Sandy admitted.

"I hate the stuff." Penelope said with a laugh. "And it tasted foul when I made it, so I can't blame Sebastian really. I always burnt the milk or didn't put the right amount of cocoa in. So darn complicated."

Sandy laughed.

"I'm awfully sorry I missed story time."

"Oh, no, I'm not worried about that. I'm worried about you."

"Yes... yes. I am too."

The words hung in the air for a few moments, Sandy considering the weight of them, the bare honesty of them.

Penelope gazed out of the window, lost in her thoughts, then pulled her handkerchief out of her pocket and wiped her eyes, real tears this time.

"Oh!" Sandy exclaimed, as if she hadn't practiced the unplanned tone of voice. "I found one of your handkerchiefs."

Penelope looked at her as Sandy pulled the handkerchief from her cardigan pocket. She passed it across to Penelope as they sat at a red light.

"I didn't expect to see this again." Penelope said, holding the delicate object in her hand with fascination.

"How did it get there?" Sandy asked. "Seems like a beautiful item to lose, so I thought I'd save it for you."

"Oh, I didn't lose it." Penelope said. "I gave it away."

"Gave it away?"

Penelope nodded. "Where did you find it?"

"At Black Rock. I've been investigating... Gurdip's widow is convinced it wasn't an accident."

Penelope swallowed. "The police closed the case."

"Mmm-hmm. Well, they never opened it really. Just a sad accident, they said."

"Sad indeed." Penelope murmured.

"Who did you give it to?" Sandy asked. "The handkerchief? There's a chance, since it was found at Black Rock, that person could be involved."

"Well, I can't really help you there." Penelope said. "I don't know who I gave it to."

"So you just gave an embossed handkerchief to a stranger?" Sandy asked with a laugh, hoping her question sounded less aggressive out loud than the thought preceding it had been.

"I saw a woman in distress, of course I gave her my handkerchief. As I say, I didn't expect to see it again."

"How did it end up at Black Rock, then? That's what I need to try and figure out."

"Well, it's fairly straightforward really. Black Rock was where I saw her, where I gave it to her."

"A mysterious woman distressed at Black Rock." Sandy said, with a shake of her head. "Cass was right, I'm looking for connections to Gurdip where there aren't any. I should just accept that Anastasia's in denial. It was clearly an accident."

"I can't comment on that, but if you're looking for a connection to Gurdip, you've found one."

"I have?"

"Of course. The woman, the distressed woman, she was with Gurdip. On the night he died."

Sandy shook her head in disbelief, forcing her attention to remain on the road. "You're kidding. I need you to tell me everything you can about what you saw."

"Oh, Sandy. It had no significance to me, I didn't really pay attention."

"Please try." Sandy pleaded.

"Okay. She was young, very young, and incredibly attractive. I was on my way back from checking on Mr Dent, and I came across them in some kind of tryst. This lady and Gurdip, not Mr Dent, I can't imagine he's been anywhere near a tryst in quite some time, poor fellow. Anyway, Gurdip had his arms around her and she was clinging to him. I, of course, looked away, but then I heard her crying, and I do believe that women should stick together, so I marched over and asked if she was okay. If she was safe, you know. She was such a beautiful mess, thick dark lashes, and a bindi on her forehead, quite intoxicating. But dreadfully upset."

"Wow." Sandy breathed.

"She was embarrassed, of course, so I offered her my handkerchief and carried on my way. That's really all I can tell you."

"You've not seen the woman before? Or since?"

Penelope shook her head. They were approaching Buxton and the roads were growing busier as they entered the town and joined commuters on their way to work.

"I'd remember her." Penelope said. "Such a beautiful girl. A sad, beautiful girl. It felt like she was falling apart on the outside just like I feel like I am on the inside sometimes."

"Oh, Penelope." Sandy said. "I'm so sorry, I should have spoke to you sooner. What can I do to help?"

"Well." Penelope said, and her voice returned to the light, cheery one Sandy was used to. She was returning to business mode, aware that they would arrive at the train station in a few minutes. "If I don't turn up for story time again, I demand that you come across to the Manor and drag me from my bed for starters."

"I was thinking more along the lines of, how can I be kind to you?"

"No need for that sort of talk, thank you very much." Penelope said. "Nobody's ever had to tiptoe around me in my life and I don't want it to start now. No, just forget we had this little talk, that's the best thing you can do for me."

"If you insist." Sandy said as she pulled up at the train station. "Now, do you have a lift home sorted or do you want me to come back? It's no trouble."

"Oh, goodness, no, you've been more than kind. Thank you, Sandy. Now, have a wonderful day!"

Penelope opened the passenger door and jumped out, then gave a mock-salute and walked away into the station.

Sandy sank down in her seat and allowed the conversation to sink in.

And she realised, as she sat with the engine running, that she knew what had happened to Gurdip.

It was time to solve the case.

14

The church was quiet and cold, and Sandy thought it was empty until she saw a slim figure sitting at the front of the pews. She gave out a low cough to announce her presence, and the figure turned, gave a smile towards her but then returned their attention forwards.

Sandy took a seat in the pew behind and gazed at the back of the man's head.

"Are you okay?" Rob Fields whispered after a few moments.

"I came to ask a favour." Sandy replied.

Rob turned in his seat, draping his arm across the back of the pew. He met her gaze with a wide smile, an eagerness to help.

"I wondered if I could borrow you." Sandy began. "I can't really explain more now."

"Now?" Rob said. "That should work, I was finished here."

"Are you sure? You looked... as if you weren't."

"I like to spend a few minutes out here with the big guy

himself." Rob said with a wink. "But a friend in need, of course, what do you need me to do?"

"Just come with me, and follow my lead."

"That I can do." Rob said. The two stood up and walked back down the aisle and out into the evening sun. Rob locked the big church door after them and then sealed it with a padlock. "Where are we headed?"

"Not far." Sandy said. She led the way, the silence between her and Rob comfortable. Creating and allowing silence for people was a big part of Rob's life, Sandy thought, and it perhaps explained how it seemed as though he moved through life at a slower pace, full of calm and reassurance. Apart from in his home, of course, where he lived like a bachelor who really needed to hire a cleaner.

Sandy's stomach grew nervous as they continued walking. She hadn't eaten all day, but had hid upstairs in the book shop, serving new and old customers and attempting to finalise her plan. A foolish plan, as the situation could escalate in any number of ways. She took a swallow and tried to steady her breathing.

"Are you ok, Sandy?" Rob asked.

"Nervous." Sandy admitted.

"But you can't tell me why." Rob said. It wasn't a question. He wasn't pleading with her to explain, but trusted that she had made the decision already. "Are you in trouble?"

"No.... no, I'm not. But someone is."

Rob nodded. "In my experience, someone always is. And is it our duty to save them? To help them? That's one of the questions we deal with in the church."

"And what's the answer?"

Rob laughed. "There's never one answer. People point to the verses that speak to them most."

"And what's your opinion?"

"I think it's quite simple. I'm a simple man really. I think if I can do a kindness, I should."

"Is that why you hired Olivia?"

"I need the help." Rob said with a shrug.

Sandy took a deep breath. "Right, we're here."

She led Rob down the path and knocked on the door. Silence. A second knock. Silence. A third knock, and the door was flung open, the occupant wild-eyed at the intrusion.

"What do you want?"

"Can we come in?" Sandy asked, her tone pointed. "We need to talk."

"I guess." And the door opened, the house darker than the outside, curtains drawn. Sandy walked ahead, seeing herself into the living room, with Rob behind her. She was glad he was there.

"Well?"

"I need you to tell me where you were on the night Gurdip died." Sandy began. Rob glanced at her, a micro-tilt of his head, then recovered his composure.

The person smiled at her request, actually smiled. A full, relieved, smile. "I thought you'd never ask."

"You were there, at Black Rock." Sandy prompted.

"I was."

"I've been trying to work it out but I need your help." Sandy admitted. The clues didn't make sense. She couldn't fit them together, piece by piece, to show the whole image.

"And why is he here?"

"To take your confession." Sandy said, simply. Rob, to his credit, didn't react at all.

"He's not a priest and I'm not a Catholic." The person said, gazing at Rob Fields.

"But..." Sandy gaped, amazed by her obvious error.

"I hear confessions regularly." Rob said, his voice calm, reassuring. "As you know, us Christians can ask forgiveness direct from our Father in prayer, but many of the congregation come to me to share mistakes. We don't call it confession, but that's what it is."

"I think you want to help me." Sandy said. "Don't you?"

"No, I want you to help me. I'm scared."

"Just tell us what happened." Sandy said, and she lowered her frame down onto a chair, an action Rob copied. Their host took a seat too, and began to cry.

"I knew he was going to Black Rock. I heard the mention of Victor Dent shooing him away and I asked him about it. He denied it. And he never lied, so I knew something was wrong. He had no reason to be on that land."

Sandy nodded, encouraging.

"That day, he had lunch at home with me, and while he was preparing the food I went through his phone. Found the messages, arranging to meet again that night."

"An affair?" Sandy asked.

Anastasia shook her head, her fingers rubbing the gold cross like a talisman. "I could have coped with that, I think. Anything but this."

"He met a woman, didn't he?"

"A girl."

"Who was she?"

The question caused Anastasia to sob, and she stood up and moved to the dining table, it's top covered with half-packed boxes. She picked up a shoe box and returned to her seat with it. Out of the box she pulled a photograph and handed it to Sandy.

The girl - and she was a girl - was beautiful. Dark eyelashes and a bindi spot. The girl from Black Rock.

"Gurdip thought I'd never find out." Anastasia said.

"And with me unable to have children, he thought it was for the best. To hide it. To hide her. She was born here, but lived in India. Then this year she came back, to find him."

"She's his daughter." Sandy breathed, the details finally slotting together.

Anastasia nodded through her tears. "I wanted a daughter more than anything in the world. Gurdip and I, we talked about it on our first date. How mad is that? Didn't feel mad then. I knew he was the love of my life, and I believe he felt the same about me."

"Why would he hide that from you?"

Anastasia gulped the tears away, choking to find her next breath. "I had a medical hysterectomy when I was young. One of the youngest cases of cervical cancer ever, I was. At the time it didn't seem like much to lose. It got rid of the cancer. It was only afterwards, I became a bit obsessed with babies. I was raging at the world really, and I focused on babies - baby girls. I became convinced that I was meant to have a daughter. I told Gurdip all this on our first date because I thought I owed him honesty. I opened up about it all; my illness, the hysterectomy, the fact I'd never have the daughter I wanted so badly. He said we could adopt, but I wanted to carry my own child. That's what hurt the most - I opened up and he didn't."

"He was trying to protect you?" Sandy offered, imagining the turmoil Gurdip must have felt on that date. Wanting to impress a young woman he had just met, or perhaps simply wanting to be sensitive to her loss. He wasn't there to explain the reasons any more, but he chose to keep quiet.

"Perhaps." Anastasia admitted. "She was a mistake. An accident. I've managed to put bits and pieces together. He'd been visiting family when it happened, just before he started University. He offered to marry the girl and bring her back here but she refused. And so that was that. He sent money, it wasn't as if he abandoned her completely. I knew he was sending money, of course, but I thought it was for his family. Well, I guess it was."

"And then she came out here to find him?"

Anastasia nodded. "This photo, she sent it with a letter, to him at the hospital in Leicester. One of his friends rang and told him there was a letter - they'd opened it, of course - a letter he needed to see. I think Gurdip knew then. I think he was always waiting for the moment it would come crashing down around him."

"Why didn't he tell you then?" Sandy asked. "You seemed to have such a strong marriage, surely you could have worked through it?"

"No." Anastasia said, her voice venomous. "How could we? How could I? She'd have been a constant reminder of what I would never have. Can you imagine it? Her coming here, calling him dad and me... well, I'd be nothing at all to her. And she'd be nothing at all to me. Just a cruel reminder."

"What happened that night?" Sandy asked.

Rob stood from his seat and moved across the room, where he sat cross-legged on the floor in front of Anastasia. "You'll feel better when you've shared this burden."

Anastasia nodded and let out a long shaky breath. "I went out to confront him, but she was there. It made me sick seeing the two of them there, together. She even looks like him. Not in the photo really, but in the flesh, the way she moved her body, the way she smiled, all of her mannerisms were his. And it made me furious."

Sandy felt her eyes water and forced herself to stare at a patch of the curtains to regain composure.

"I couldn't speak to him with her there, I knew she'd think I was pathetic. And maybe he'd have to choose between us and he'd choose her. I couldn't stand the thought of that. So I waited, and eventually she started crying. She was screaming at him, and that's what did it really. I realised she was angry too, and it hit me how much he'd let her down. I hated him then, and I'm ashamed to admit it. He'd had the thing I wanted most, all along, and he'd abandoned it. Her."

"He made that choice for you."

"I didn't care. The woman from the Manor walked by then, and she gave the girl a handkerchief, and the girl left after that. Gurdip just stood there, looking out over Black Rock, and I went out to confront him."

Anastasia closed her eyes and her fists clenched as her mind relived the night. "I told him I knew and he didn't try to deny it. He was scared of me, I could see that. I must have looked like a madwoman. I was so angry, and soaked through. I kept getting closer and closer and..."

"It's okay." Rob murmured.

"He was backing away from me, but I was too angry to see that. He was backing away and I was screaming questions at him and he wouldn't answer me. He wouldn't bloody answer. I kept screaming, begging him, to give me answers. I deserved answers! And he wouldn't even give me those. So I shoved him. I pushed him in the chest. I just wanted him to realise, he had to talk to me. He had to explain. But I shoved him and he went over, he went over the ledge and I knew, I knew straightaway that was it, he was... he was dead."

Anastasia collapsed into tears, her breath ragged. She covered her face with her hands and her whole body shook as the sobs racked through her.

"It wasn't even investigated. You were the one suggesting he hadn't fallen. Why would you do that?"

Anastasia removed her hands and scoffed. "Look at the trouble secrets have caused. I need to own up to what happened, but I didn't have the courage to hand myself in. I needed someone else to work it out. It had to be you, Sandy."

Sandy let out a sigh. "You know we have to call the police."

"I know. I've been preparing for that. I redid my Will so the house proceeds can go to her. I'm ready."

Sandy nodded and pulled her phone from her handbag.

"Sandy." Rob said. "Make the call in the other room, please. I'd like to spend a few moments praying with Anastasia."

Sandy nodded and left the room.

Anastasia watched her, her eyes red raw. "Thank you, Sandy."

15

*A*nastasia's house sold quickly once word spread, and the villagers' bets were on it being an investment buyer with an interest in ghoulish properties.

Anastasia herself made full admissions in interview when the police arrived, and Jim Slaughter got to announce the news himself to a crowd of journalists outside the local police station. Dorie's head had been almost too big to fit inside Books and Bakes since.

Manslaughter.

Not murder.

Not that it would make much difference to Anastasia, who had lost the person she loved most in the world.

The mysterious daughter, with the dark eyelashes and Bindi spot, never made an appearance in Waterfell Tweed, although rumours began that she had attended the funeral. Sandy put those down to the usual village gossip until Rob Fields himself, who had led the service, agreed that he believed she had quietly taken a seat in the back pew and left before the service had finished.

"Penny for them?" Cass asked, looking down into Sandy's eyes. Sandy smiled and shook her head.

"Am I done?"

"You certainly are, I threw in a cheeky five minutes more than I should have but the next customer'll be here in a minute." Cass said. She had offered Sandy a massage, perhaps realising that Sandy wasn't cut out for the pain of eyebrow waxing.

"That was Heaven." Sandy admitted, although she wasn't sure if she'd stayed awake for the whole thing.

"You'd got some real knots, you know. You carry lots of stress. It's not good for you."

"Tell me about it." Sandy scoffed.

"I'm serious. You need to start having more fun, lady. In fact..."

"Oh, dear, I should have known there was a motive. You're not going to try and get me to run a 5k with you again, are you? Because that is not my idea of fun."

"No! I couldn't agree more about the running, by the way, it's torture. I was actually going to see if you and Tom fancy a night out."

"Hmm... tell me more." Sandy asked, suspicious.

"Tonight." Cass said, eyelashes fluttering. "Bomber's asked me out, and he suggested you guys could join us... like a double date?"

"A double date?" Sandy asked, raising her eyebrows. "Really?"

"See what I mean. Anyone needs a murder investigating and you're all over it, but a fun night out and you're suspicious. You're officially insane."

Sandy let out a laugh. "You know what?"

Cass glanced at her.

"You're right. I'm sorry. Let me speak to Tom, but if

he's free, sure, we'd love to. And if he's not free, I'm not coming alone to play gooseberry so don't even suggest it."

"Oh, I won't, don't worry." Cass said as the salon door opened. A well-presented woman of an unguessable age, with a small dog stuffed in an oversized handbag, removed her sunglasses and took a seat in the reception area. Sandy glanced at Cass but said nothing.

"I'll let you know. Thanks again." Sandy called as she left her best friend to see to her next client.

**

To Sandy's surprise when she popped into The Tweed and raised the idea, Tom loved it.

"We should go out more often. This is a great idea."

"You heard the bit where Cass and Bomber are there too, yeah?"

"And?"

"Well, just, nothing I guess. I didn't expect you to fancy it."

Tom rolled his eyes. "It's a night out with you, of course I fancy it. And it'll be fun to get to know Cass better, she's been a bit of a ballbuster to me but I think she's starting to warm to me."

"Bomber can be... interesting."

"Sandy, wasn't the guy practically your second best friend at one point?"

"Has he been talking to you?" Sandy asked.

"I'm a barman. Everyone talks to me." Tom said with a cheeky grin.

Sandy threw him her best withering look. "I don't want to know what he's told you."

"It doesn't matter if you do, I couldn't tell you anyway."

"Excuse me?"

"Client confidentiality." Tom said, his expression serious.

"Client confidentiality? I don't think that applies to your conversations with drunk men."

"Better to be safe than sorry." Tom said.

"You're infuriating." Sandy said.

He leaned over the bar and planted a kiss on her lips. "And you love me."

"Yes I do." Sandy said with a grin. "I'll see you later then?"

**

The evening flew by in a whirl of old stories, told by the three of them while Tom listened and laughed along with an indulgence that made Sandy adore him even more. The wine flowed freely and although they all agreed the food was overpriced and overrated, they didn't let that dampen their spirits. Bomber insisted on remaining sober so that he could drive them all home, and he spoke openly about his struggles finding work.

"I always need bar staff." Tom said.

"Really?"

"Absolutely. Especially now I've got Sandy in my life. We're like ships that pass in the night with her working day time and my busiest times being evening." Tom explained.

Sandy felt her stomach flip at his words. She had felt the

same way, but hadn't vocalised it as she didn't see a solution. He was a pub landlord, it went with the territory.

"Don't suppose you've got any experience in the pub trade?" Tom asked.

"Well... a little." Bomber said.

Cass elbowed his side. "Tell him the truth."

"I used to own a chain of bars." Bomber said with a shrug.

"Oh wow, you'd probably be bored stiff in my little pub then."

"Don't be too impressed, they went under so I've hardly got the magic touch."

"He's told me all about it and I think he just expanded too quick." Cass said. She had quite the business brain underneath her war paint.

"She needs to be my business partner when I get back up and running." Bomber said with a grin. He gazed at Cass with admiration. "Beauty and brains. I tell you what, Tom, you and me are lucky guys."

"I'll drink to that." Tom said. He raised his glass and gave a tipsy grin towards Sandy, who help up her own glass and winked at Cass. Finally, they managed to align all of their glasses, which seemed to be much harder than it should have been and may or may not have been due to the wine they'd consumed, and chinked their glasses.

"To beauty and brains!" Bomber called, a little too loud. The group on the next table turned to see what the fuss was about.

"To old friends." Sandy said.

"To second chances." Cass said, her voice thick with emotion.

The three of them, and the people on the next table, all looked at Tom, eager for his own toast.

"To my new pub manager, Bomber!" Tom cried out with a grin. "You're hired so I can spend more time with this beautiful woman... and don't worry, that's not the wine talking."

THE END

WANT MORE COZY CONTENT?

If you're a lover of cozy mysteries, join my VIP Reader List.

Every Thursday, I send out an eMail packed with updates on my writing progress and life, plus special cozy mystery offers, free gifts, exclusive content and more.

Sign up now:

http://monamarple.com/wt6/

ABOUT THE AUTHOR

Mona Marple is a mother, author and coffee enthusiast. She is creator of the Waterfell Tweed cozy mystery series and the Mystic Springs paranormal cozy mystery series.

You can see all of her books at author.to/MonaMarple

When she isn't busy writing a cozy mystery, she's probably curled up somewhere warm reading one.

She lives in England with her husband and daughter.

Connect with Mona:
www.MonaMarple.com
mona@monamarple.com